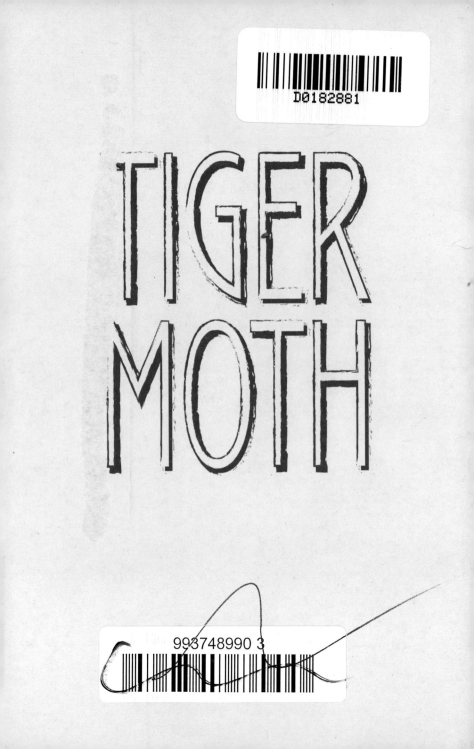

TIGER MOTH

Other titles by Suzi Moore

LEXILAND

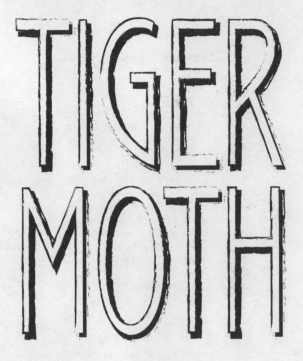

TIGER MOTH

Suzi Moore

SIMON AND SCHUSTER

First published in Great Britain in 2014 by Simon & Schuster UK Ltd,
1st Floor, 222 Gray's Inn Road
London, WC1X 8HB
A CBS COMPANY

PB ISBN: 978-0-85707-510-9
eBook ISBN: 978-0-85707-511-6

1 3 5 7 9 10 8 6 4 2

Simon & Schuster Australia, Sydney
Simon & Schuster India, New Delhi

A CIP catalogue record for this book is available from the British Library.
This book is a work of fiction. Names, characters, places and incidents are either
the product of the author's imagination or are used fictitiously. Any resemblance
to actual people living or dead, events or locales is entirely coincidental.
Printed and bound by CPI Group (UK) Ltd, Croydon, CR0 4YY

Typeset by Hewer Text UK Ltd, Edinburgh
Printed and bound in Great Britain by CPI Group (UK) Ltd, Croydon, CR0 4YY

www.simonandschuster.co.uk
www.simonandschuster.com.au

For George Emmanuel Moore with love x x x

I don't know why he threw the thing so far, but I love a challenge so I went straight after it. I think I almost flew off the rocks. I moved faster than my legs have ever moved and I didn't take my eyes off it for a second. I could hear all five of them shouting my name, but I kept on going. Further and further I went. At first it felt easy, but then it started to get harder and harder. Something wasn't right. But I was not going to give up. I would never give up; my best friend says I'm the most determined thing he's ever met.

Their voices were getting fainter now and I started to panic. I started to think I wouldn't make it after all and suddenly my legs didn't want to move any more. I think that the last thing I heard was, 'Oh no! Somebody do something!'

And, as a silence surrounded me, I knew that it was too late.

1

Alice

I'm not like you. I'm not like everyone else. I wasn't born. I was chosen.

Mum and Dad say this: 'You were special. We chose you and then we took you home.'

Well, it was sort of like that.

Ten years ago, I arrived in the world at five past six on a very rainy November morning, but, unlike all of the other babies who had been born that day, I didn't go home with my real mother. She went back to her life (I think) and I was taken somewhere else. I was driven out to the countryside to a huge house with lots of other wriggling babies.

Mum says that she had wished and hoped that, one day, she would be lucky enough to have a little girl to love, and in December they got a telephone call to say that I was waiting for them. Mum says that it was the best day of her life. Dad says he was so happy he cried and laughed all at the same time. Sometimes I imagine that, when they arrived at the house with all the babies, they were shown into a room which had rows and rows of cots. I like to think that they walked up and down the aisles of wriggling, gurgling babies and when they got to my cot they knew that I was their daughter. I like to think that even though I was only four weeks old I saw my mum and dad and I knew straight away that they were the ones for me too.

Mum and Dad say that I am the best thing that has ever happened to them, that I was the missing piece in the Richardson family jigsaw and that I was the perfect fit. They say that life at Culver Manor just got better and better when they brought me home. I was the happiness that took all the sad feeling away. I was the laughter that brought the old house back to life.

And it's a very old house. Culver Manor is where my father was born and his father before him and his father before him, and the main part of the house was built when Henry the Eighth was King of England. There are ten bedrooms, four sitting rooms and a hall that's a bit like a church inside with beautiful stained-glass windows that shimmer in the sunlight. There's a library too and it's even bigger than the one in the village, but I'm not really supposed to go in there on my own because there are lots of very special books which Dad says are valuable and that no one should touch.

There are tons of other places to mess around in and, even though I have a really big playroom, most of the time I think my bedroom is the best room in the house. It's kind of extra special because it's at the top of a 'secret' staircase. There's a really grand staircase in the hallway, but the 'secret' stairs are wooden and spiral upwards to the first floor where there's a little window shaped like a diamond (my dad is always leaving his reading glasses on that window ledge and forgetting all about them). Between my bedroom and my parents' room is a very long hallway with three windows that all have seats that you can snuggle up on and hide behind the long, heavy, red velvet curtains. When my cousin Florence comes to stay, we always camp out on the window seats, pull the curtains closed and share ghost stories.

Apart from my bedroom and the window seats, my other favourite place is the garden. It has loads of different places to hide too. There's a kitchen garden where we grow all our own vegetables, a big pond with a summer house, a tennis court and a large walled garden with lots and lots of roses. They flower all through the summer: palest pinks and brightest reds, climbing roses with tiny white buds and lilac ones with petals so fat and heavy that they droop down from the wall as though they're too tired to stand up tall. They fill the garden with a delicate perfume and if I leave my bedroom window open I can smell them as I lie in bed. I love the old cherry tree which has a swing on it and you can swing back and forth, looking down the garden and out to sea. When I was little, Dad used to let me sit on his lap as we swung our feet as high as we dared.

I know that Culver Manor is a very special place, and I'm really lucky to live there. Sometimes I invite my friends round and they can never believe how huge it is. They think it's like something out of a book.

The one place in the house that I'm not allowed to go on my own is the attic. I'm only allowed up there when Dad or Mum is with me. Last week I went up with Dad, so he could find some old photographs, and he got me a little stool to stand on so that I could see out of the really high-up windows that look out to sea. I could see all the way across the Bristol Channel to the Black Mountains in Wales even though we live in Somerset.

While he was searching through piles of dusty boxes, I found a little door in the corner of the attic and when I opened it I got quite a surprise. It was a small room, no bigger than a cupboard, with walls covered in maps and posters of footballers. Tucked under the little window was a table and three chairs. On the middle of the table there was an abandoned model aeroplane, with paints and paintbrushes next to it, so that it almost looked as though it was waiting for someone to come back and finish it.

I must have stood in that strange little room for quite a while, just staring at all the dusty little aeroplanes which hung down from the ceiling on bits of string. I lifted my hand up towards one that was kind of grey, but when I blew the dust off I saw it was actually painted bright yellow. I couldn't believe that I didn't know this room existed.

I didn't hear Dad walk in, but, when I looked up and saw him, his face was really strange. I asked what the matter was, but he just shook his head. Then I noticed that the backs of the chairs all had a different letter painted on them. T, D and K. I knew the D was for my dad, David, and the T must have been for his brother, Tom, but what did the K stand for? When I asked Dad, he shook his head again and pushed the three chairs over to the far corner, stacking them up neatly so the letters were hidden. He said we should go back downstairs and pulled me towards the door, but as he did something caught my eye. One of the posters on the wall was peeling away and I swear I saw a sort of drawing underneath it. Was it a map? I couldn't be sure and as I followed Dad back downstairs I kept wondering about the secrets of the small room. Whose chair was that? What did the K stand for? What was the drawing on the wall?

Apart from the attic, there's one more place that I'm forbidden to go.

Culver Cove.

The vale where we live is green and beautiful. The shoreline is made up of two large beaches which curve along the coast like the number three, but they're not sandy beaches. They're all stone. There are big stones, very big stones, medium-sized stones, small stones and ever so teeny-weeny stones. And each one is very different. Some are blue. Some are grey. Some are palest pink. Some stones have a white stripe. Some stones have two white stripes. Some are round. Some are oval. Some are really very flat indeed. But all of them are the same in one respect alone. They're all very smooth. Smoothest of smooth. But the beach at Culver Cove is sandy. It's the only sandy beach and it can only be reached from our garden along a dark, dangerous, winding footpath, but I have never been.

Dad says that years ago there was a landslide and the footpath is so covered with rocks and mud that it's too difficult to walk along. If I ever ask why we can't clear the path, my dad will pull a funny face, tell a silly joke or ask me to name all the planets. The last time I asked it was the day before his birthday and even though it was September it was really hot. '*Can we go to the cove, Daddy? Can we, please? We could have a birthday swim?*' I had begged, but my dad looked really, *really* weird. I waited for ages for him to answer and he and Mum kept giving each other strange looks.

'David,' Mum had said, tipping her head to one side and stroking his cheek. 'Maybe we should tell Alice the . . .' but my dad suddenly pulled away from Mum's gentle hands and looked quite cross.

'No,' he said in an angry sort of voice. 'Leave the past alone, Sophie.'

Mum opened her mouth to say something and I swear that as he left the room there were tears in Daddy's eyes.

In the end Mum said, 'Let's make your daddy a carrot cake for his birthday instead. Why don't you come and help me?' And I did. I love carrot cake the most. I think it's my favourite food. That and watermelon. Mum always makes me and Dad a carrot cake on our birthday.

Even though my birthday is on November 8th, every year on December 6th we have a family celebration too. We call it our family birthday and I think it's pretty great because I get presents then and eighteen days later it's Christmas. Everyone at school says I'm lucky, but one time my cousin Florence told me that no one else has a family birthday so I asked her why.

She looked at me and rolled her eyes. 'Because, Alice, I live with my real family, silly.'

Then she sort of laughed and took a bite out of her apple. I wasn't really sure I knew what she meant, but that night, when we all sat down for dinner, I looked up at Mum and asked her where my real family was.

She spat out her drink, started coughing and Dad dropped his knife and fork so that they sort of clattered on to the plate. They looked at me and it was as if they were angry or really upset, and when Mum spoke again she was sort of crying.

'This *is* your real family, Alice,' she said. 'Your real family is the one that loves and cares for you the most.'

She looked so upset that I got up from my seat and gave her the biggest cuddle I could. I didn't want her to be sad. I didn't want her to cry any more. I wanted her to smile. And she did. So, even though I sometimes have so many questions about my other mother that it feels as though my head will explode, I didn't ask again. But I didn't feel really sad or anything like that because my family is the best family in the world.

Well, it was.

Everything was just perfect until it wasn't.

2

Alice

Everything was perfect until February. Then something happened which changed everything. I remember the day really well because it had been raining all night and the wind was so loud it kind of woke me up, but in the morning there wasn't a single cloud in the sky. We sat down for breakfast at the kitchen table. It's a long rectangular one with a big wooden top and, if you run your hand along the honey-coloured wood, it feels kind of warm. Mum says it's really old, but I like it because it smells special. It makes the whole kitchen smell a bit like a forest.

I sat down in my chair by the window that looks down across the garden and out to sea. The sea was dark blue that day and I could tell it was still windy outside because the waves were rolling along the shore in white frothy peaks. Just as I took a big gulp of milk, my mum set down a plate of warm croissants and smiled at me.

'We've got some amazing news,' she said.

Dad took her hand in his and turned to me. 'Alice, you're going to have a little sister.'

I looked at them and grinned.

'Really?' I said, jumping up from the table. I'd always wanted a little brother or sister, like most of my friends had, and I immediately thought about the big house in the country where Mum and Dad had collected me from when I was a tiny baby.

The special place where they'd chosen me from all the others.

'Yippee!' I shouted. 'I've always wanted a sister.'

They smiled.

'Mum, can I choose? Can I choose which one?'

They looked funny. They both tried to say something and then Dad leaned towards Mum and lifted up the bottom of her jumper and patted her rounded tummy.

'No, silly. Mum is going to have a baby.'

I didn't understand.

'What do you mean?' I asked.

Mum opened up her handbag, pulled out a small white envelope and passed it to me.

'Look inside.'

I pulled out a black-and-white photograph. It wasn't like any picture I had seen before. It was sort of blurred and I could only see two roundish black-and-white shapes. I looked up and frowned. 'What is it?'

'That's your little sister. Look.' Mum pointed at the larger round shape. 'That's her head and those,' she said, pointing at the tiny white dots, 'are her hands.'

I looked down at the picture again. Now that I knew what it was supposed to be, I could almost make out the shape of a teeny-weeny body. I really could see a head, hands and feet.

'By the end of August you'll have a little sister,' Mum said.

I watched Dad rub Mum's tummy and they both smiled at each other again, but I felt funny. It wasn't a good feeling. It made my stomach sort of twist and turn. Mum reached her hand across the table to mine.

'Well?' she said, stroking my fingers.

I snatched my hand from hers.

'Well, what?' I said angrily.

They both looked shocked and I don't know why, but I suddenly pushed my chair away from the table and stood up.

'Alice, don't you have anything to say?'

I sighed and looked down at my dad's freckly face.

'Is there anything you want to ask us?' Mum said.

I opened my mouth to speak, but the words didn't come out. I didn't have anything to say. In fact, I didn't have anything to say that day or the day after that or the day after that.

And I haven't spoken since. Not a word. Not a yes or a no or a please or a thank you. I nod my head, I shake my head and most of the time I just sigh and frown at them. Since then I spend a lot of time thinking about that black-and-white blurry picture of my soon-to-be little sister. I think about the day I was chosen and most of the time I try to imagine what my other mother looks like.

After two weeks of not speaking, Mum and Dad took me to a special doctor's, but he told them there was nothing really wrong with me. So I had to go to another kind of doctor. She spoke to Mum and Dad while I sat in the waiting room. After a while, they opened the door and I had to go inside. I sat silently while she asked me lots of questions and then the doctor lady gave me a notebook. She said if I didn't want to talk, if I felt I couldn't speak, perhaps I could write instead.

When we went back to school, my mum and dad had to have a 'really big talk' with the teachers. The children at school teased me for a bit. Actually, some of them were a bit mean, but after a while they just ignored me.

It's like I don't exist.

3

Zack

My dad used to be a stuntman.

I'm not kidding. I don't mind if you don't believe me because at first I used to think he was joking. My friends at school thought I was making it up. 'Zack,' they'd say, 'you're talking rubbish.' Then, one day in the school holidays, my dad took me to a place in London where they make movies. It was like an enormous garage and inside there were lots of pretend rooms and pretend streets. Each one was different, but they all looked very real. It was awesome. I met a woman who does all the make-up. Dad let me sit in her special chair and I was allowed to have a sort of monster face made. When Mum saw me, she said I frightened the pants off her, but I thought it was hilarious.

So, when I went back to school, I showed my friends the photographs I'd taken. I showed them the pictures of Dad so they could see with their own eyes that he really was a stunt-man. He really was the man who jumped out of planes, off the top of buildings and out of burning cars for none other than James Bond.

Which I think is probably the coolest and most interesting job that a dad can have. Ask your dad. I bet he'll agree.

Mum says that Dad wasn't scared of anything at all. Apart from rats. He hated rats. Which was why I wasn't allowed a pet rat for my tenth birthday, but I did get something even better. I got a dog. A chocolate-brown puppy with the biggest eyes you ever saw and we all decided that he looked just like an otter so that was what we called him.

The one thing my dad really loved to do was fly. He always said it was his first love. When he was sixteen, he flew across the English Channel all by himself. Sometimes I would go with him to the airfield at the weekend and we would polish his little yellow plane so much that you could see your face in the wings. I loved that yellow plane. I used to sit in the cockpit and Dad showed me how it worked. He took me up in it eight times and he told me that, when I was old enough, he would let me fly it myself and, if I could just learn how to hold the brushes more carefully, if I could keep my hands still, I might be able to make the miniature planes like he could too. Mum said that the two of us spent so much time talking about planes and cleaning, polishing and fixing the little yellow plane that I could probably already fly it all by myself with a blindfold on. Dad said that if I was anything like him I probably could.

Then, one day, almost exactly sixteen months ago on May 29th, we went to watch my dad perform his aeroplane tricks at a special show where lots of stuntmen and women came from all over the world to amaze the crowds with their Daredevil Show. We drove from our house in London to Sussex in my dad's brand-new red sports car which had one of those roofs that you can take down. By the time we arrived, Mum's hair was kind of blown in every direction so that it looked like a seagull was nesting in it. I remember that I was really excited and I just couldn't wait to see what sort of tricks my dad was going to perform. We watched the crowds getting bigger and bigger and, when they knew it was time for my dad, the James Bond stuntman, they cheered and cheered.

I heard the little yellow plane chug past the crowds and I watched as Dad sped up down the runway and took off. Do you know the song 'Those Magnificent Men in their Flying Machines'? If you don't, ask a grown-up. I bet you anything they can sing it for you. It goes a bit like this:

Those magnificent men in their flying machines,
They go up, tiddly up, up,
They go down, tiddly down, down.
Up,
Down,
Flying around,
Looping the loop and defying the ground.

That afternoon we watched as my dad went up, up, up. We shouted and waved as he went down, down, down. I shouted, 'I love you, Dad!' as he looped the loop not once but three times. Then he went down, down, down, but the little yellow plane did not defy the ground. It went down, down, down, all the way to the ground, where it became a ball of yellow and orange flames.

That was how my dad died.

We didn't have a funeral where everyone cries and dresses up in black. We had a massive party at our house which went on all weekend. Mum said it was a party to celebrate Dad's amazing life. The house was so full of people that you could hardly get up the stairs without having to climb over someone. And everyone kept telling me how great my dad was, how everyone had loved him and that there was no one else in the world that could do stunts as good as he could. But it didn't feel very amazing to me.

If he was such an amazing stuntman, why couldn't he have landed the little yellow plane properly like he normally did? Why did he smash the plane into the ground? I want to ask Mum about it, but I'm too scared. She gets a bit upset when I ask about Dad and I hate to see her cry. Sometimes I fall asleep to the sound of her sobbing, and quite a few times I've woken up and she's asleep in the bunk bed below mine, but I don't mind. The last time she did that I went downstairs, made her a cup of tea and a piece of toast, although I did spill quite a bit of the tea on the carpet and I forgot to put her three sugars in, but she smiled loads when she saw the breakfast in bed.

So far I haven't cried at all. I keep waiting for it to happen. Mum says I have to be really brave, just like Dad was, but I don't think I could ever be as brave as him. Really I keep waiting for Dad to suddenly burst through the door, but that hasn't happened either.

Mum says in a way we're 'lucky duckies' because we have each other, and my mum isn't like any of the other mums I know. She's much younger than all my friends' mums, but sometimes I wish she'd wear less embarrassing clothes. She once told me that she hadn't planned to have babies or anything like that. She wasn't really interested in changing nappies and stuff, so I was a bit of an 'accident'. But then she told me that her and Dad always said that if all accidents were as wonderful as me they'd fall over on purpose all day long.

After it happened, Mum wanted us to go on holiday to a tiny island in the Caribbean for Christmas. She said it might not feel so sad if we went away instead of being at the house without Dad because, unlike all of my friends from school, I don't have any grandparents. My dad never knew his mum and dad because he grew up in one of those homes where lots of children with no parents live. My mum's mum died before I was born and her dad died before I had learnt to talk. Mum says I did meet him, but I don't remember. So, even though Mum has lots of friends, we don't have any family left now, and Christmas would have just been the two of us which would have felt a bit weird.

The trip sounded exciting and we were supposed to fly there on a massive plane, but the day before I started feeling weird. I kept asking Mum if we'd be safe in the big plane and she had to keep telling me we'd be OK. I actually felt sick when I went to bed and every time I closed my eyes I saw Dad's little yellow plane as it burst into flames. Mum let Otter sleep on my bed that night, but I still had the world's most horrid dream that our plane crashed into the ocean and we were surrounded by great white sharks. I woke up sweating and panting for breath.

At the airport it got worse. The noise from the planes and the crowds of people rushing this way and that way made me feel dizzier and dizzier until I felt like I couldn't catch my breath. I wanted to shout: 'I don't want to go! What if we crash too?' I wanted to cry, but I wouldn't let myself. Dad always said that you should always do the thing that scares you the most, but I wasn't as brave as him and I knew in that moment I never could be.

As we stood in the queue to board, I saw the burning plane once more and it was too much; the Coke bottle fell from my hand and I turned and ran. Well, I ran as far as a security guard would let me which wasn't that far really. He grabbed hold of my rucksack and I fell to the ground and banged my head. For some reason I kicked out at him and, even though I didn't really kick him that hard, Mum was more cross about that than us missing our plane. She was even angrier when I refused to say sorry.

'He wasn't a security guard, Zack! He was a policeman! You can get into big trouble for that sort of thing, you know. Whatever would your dad say?'

That was the moment I swore at her. It just kind of came out really, really loudly. And it wasn't just any old swear word, it was the worst kind. Mum stood there, staring at me, and didn't speak to me all the way back home.

That night I lay awake, thinking about the last holiday we'd all been on together. We'd flown to a tiny island which had white sandy beaches and turquoise water. The day before we left we went sailing on a beautiful white yacht. The three of us ate a lunch of barbecued lobsters and afterwards Dad and I both jumped off the back of the boat to swim with the turtles. That was one of the best and most fun days I've ever had, but thinking about it now just made me feel sad. Because I won't ever get to do that again, will I?

When I had to go back to school, everyone was really nice to me, but for some reason that made me feel worse. It was a feeling that sort of hovered over me. It was a feeling that got worse when I saw my friend's dad cheering him on at our school football match. It was a feeling that made me want to shout or cry or something even worse when I saw all the other dads collecting my friends the last day of term. And when Mum took me to the cinema I noticed that all the other children were with both their mum and dad. It felt as though everyone had their dad but me. I wanted the feeling to go away, but it just stayed and stayed.

21

A week after the Easter holidays I came home from school and Mum was sitting at the kitchen table with two very serious-looking men who I'd never seen before. They wore grey suits and grey expressions, and I could see that Mum had been crying. They were talking about money and the house, and I heard Mum say, 'That can't be right. He would have remembered.' Then she turned round and saw me standing in the doorway and told me to go upstairs. I wanted to stay and see what they were talking about, but she just shut the door.

That night Mum made me my favourite dinner and as I slurped on the spaghetti and meatballs she told me the bad news. I looked up at her and watched her twist her black hair round her finger, then she took a deep breath.

'Zack, those men that were here earlier . . . well, the thing is . . . we've run out of money.'

I kind of frowned a bit. I didn't get it.

'We're in a bit of a mess money-wise. We're going to have to sell the house.'

She started to cry and turned to face the window so that I couldn't see. I still didn't understand. We didn't have any money? We were going to have to sell the house? It didn't make sense at all. We'd always had plenty of money. We lived in a nice house on one of the best streets. We had three cars and nearly always had a holiday each year, and my school was one of those that you had to pay to go to.

'Zack, honey, it seems like your dad was . . .'

I waited. She sighed and rubbed her eyes so that she smudged the make-up down her cheeks.

'Those men, well, they had some bad news. How can I explain this? When you work, when you have a job and earn a living, you don't get to just keep all the money you earn.'

'Why not?' I said, frowning properly this time.

'You have to give a bit, a rather big bit, to the taxman. For the rest of the country. So that we can have schools and hospitals and build roads and things. The more money you earn, the more taxes you have to pay and your dad sort of forgot to do that. So now we owe the tax people money, a lot more money than we have in the bank.' She sat down next to me and kissed my cheek. 'Zack, we're going to have to sell all the things we have. The cars, the house and even then we'll be . . .' She sighed and shook her head. 'Our life is going to be very different from now on.'

And it was.

Our life was about to become completely different.

4

Zack

Over the next three months we sold everything we had. Firstly Mum sold all her jewellery. The diamond necklace she got for her birthday, the ruby ring she got for Christmas and the special bracelet that Dad and I had picked out for their anniversary. She sold all the paintings in the house so that the walls were left with these big, square, empty patches. She sold all the antique furniture so that we only had two mattresses and our clothes lay in piles on the floor. She sold Dad's sports car, the jeep and the silver Mini Cooper so that we had to walk to school.

Debbie the housekeeper stopped coming to the house so that it started to get messier and messier. The fridge that had always been bursting with my favourite food and drink became emptier and emptier until last night I found one mini Babybel and a vanilla yoghurt. Our house had always been filled with colour and music and new people hanging out in the kitchen, but when they came and took everything away we stopped getting any visitors and our home felt empty and strange.

It's already July; it's been months since Mum told me the bad news and next week will be my last week at school and I'm already dreading it. Mum doesn't want anyone to know what's really happening, so I can't tell anyone. She says that she doesn't want anyone to feel sorry for her and that we have to start our lives again, but I don't want to start my life again. I want to go back to how it was before. Sixteen months ago, before Dad died.

Our house is filled with photographs of Dad and normally I look at one of the pictures and say hello to him. I'll say hello to him bungee jumping off the Eiffel Tower or good-night to him in a suit at a fancy party, but last night I didn't bother. The day Dad died was really sad, but it felt as though he was still here. Now I really wish he was so I could ask him why. I wish I could properly tell him off for leaving me and Mum in such a horrible mess because sometimes I can feel really angry with my stupid dad and his idiotic 'forgetting to pay the taxman'.

When I woke up this morning, I looked around at my bedroom which used to be full of cool stuff, but was now nearly empty. My computer, fridge, guitar, TV, model planes, they were all gone. I looked at the empty walls, the piles of clothes on the floor and saw that Otter had made a new basket for himself in a mountain of towels. I leaned forward and stroked his ears; he loves that. He loves being with me the most and he hates being by himself. The first time we left him in the house on his own he chewed the legs off Mum's special sculpture, chewed the cushions on the sofa and weed all over the new carpet. Dad used to say that Otter was just like me, that we both hated to be by ourselves for longer than five minutes. It's kind of true, although I don't chew cushions.

I got up off my mattress and thought about the week ahead. The last week at school with all my friends. Louis is my best mate; we've known each other since primary school and we do everything together, but since I told him I was leaving London he and Ed have been hanging out a lot more than they usually do. I phoned him last night, but the two of them had gone to the cinema together. Part of me thinks that Lou will forget about me once I'm gone, but I'm trying not to think about that.

I've been wondering about what kind of school I'll go to in September and what everyone will be like. I've never been the new kid before and it kind of scares me; it makes me feel like that might be the worst thing about all of this. It makes me feel terrible. In fact, ever since I found out we were going to have to move, I've been pretty miserable.

When Mum told me about selling the house, I wasn't sure where we'd go. Then she showed me a photograph of our new home, the little house where she had grown up.

Not only did I have to move out of my home, leave my school and all my friends, but we were going to leave London too and it made me so cross that I threw the last can of Diet Coke across the room and kicked the bin on the way out. She told me to come back and sit down, but I wouldn't; instead I just hovered by the door. She came closer and tried to put her hand on my shoulder, but I just shrugged her off me, moved away and leaned against the fridge, folding my arms across my chest. She sat down at the kitchen table and opened a shoe-box full of photographs that I didn't really recognise.

'Look,' she said. 'I was about your age when this was taken.'

I turned away and sighed, but she moved the photo right underneath my nose so I had to look. It was of a row of three white cottages with a group of people outside the middle one. There were two fair-haired boys that looked so alike, both of them smiling in the sunshine; the younger one looked as though the other had just told him the funniest joke.

I recognised Mum straight away. She was sitting on the wall next to the tallest boy, her arm round his waist, a gap-toothed grin lighting up his freckly face. Standing on the wall next to Mum was another girl with long blonde hair, her hands on her hips, her cheeks puffed out and her eyes tightly shut. Standing at the gate and looking back across at them was a tall man with a rounded tummy. His black hair stuck out from underneath a cap, his hands were the size of dinner plates and resting on his foot was a tiny black dog. I turned away, not looking at the rest of the people in the photo. I didn't want to see any more. I didn't care.

'That's my dad,' Mum said with a sad smile. 'He didn't have many things. He wasn't interested in money, but when he died he left a will saying that he wanted his only grandson, you, to have his cottage. It's yours.'

'Why?' I said angrily. 'I don't want the stupid cottage! Can't we sell it then we'd have some money? Then we could stay here!' I shouted at her.

'I can't, Zack. At the moment that cottage is all we have and if I owned it, if it was my house, the bank or the taxman would take it away from me and sell it to pay off Dad's debts. But because it belongs to you it means that they can't touch it. You can't sell it until you're eighteen.'

Eighteen! That was six years from now. That was forever.

'Zack, please. Try and understand. We're really lucky. Exmoor is a wonderful place to grow up. You're going to love it, Zack. The cottage is right on the beach so you can do lots of water sports; you'll like that. If it wasn't for Granddad, you and I would be homeless.'

Homeless? The word scared me. It made me think of those people you see outside the Tube.

Mum keeps saying how sorry she is, but I'm so cross that I've started being a bit mean to her. I can't help it. I try and be nice, like when I saw her packing all of Dad's old clothes into big brown boxes I saw she was sort of crying. I went to get some tissues, but as my hand reached out to the tissue box I caught sight of my empty bedroom, the miserable, lonely mattress, and I swiped the box on to the floor.

So I'm twelve years old and I own a cottage that I don't even want to see, never mind live in, but I don't have a choice. I have a right to be mad at Mum, don't I? I have a right to be mega-angry at Dad, don't I? I'm starting to think I sort of hate him and I know I already HATE the stupid cottage by the sea.

5

Alice

Do you look a bit like your mum? Or does someone always tell you that you look just like your dad? Maybe there's another relative in your family who has the same hair colour or the same blue eyes? Perhaps you're really good at playing the piano, just like your mum? I'm not. I don't look anything like my mum or my dad. I don't look like my aunt or my uncle.

My mum has golden hair and eyes that are almost grey. Mine are not. My dad has reddish- blond hair and freckles all over his face, his arms, his hands, and his eyes are as blue as a swimming pool. Mine are not. My mum has skin that is so pale you can see the veins in her arms, and every summer she has to wear a hat and lots of suncream. So does Dad. So does his little sister, so do my cousins, but I don't. I don't look like them at all. My name is Alice Isabella Richardson, but I don't look like anyone in the Richardson family.

My hair isn't blonde or red or even brown, it's black. Blackest black. My skin isn't pinkish or pale or even freckly. My eyes aren't grey, blue, green or anything in between. They're darkest brown. Dad says I have eyes that are shaped like large almonds and Mum says they're the colour of melting chocolate. She says I have the thickest spidery eyelashes that she has ever seen and that when I cry they sort of stick together like the bristles of a paintbrush. Mum is tall, very tall. They both are. Tall and skinny. And me? I'm the smallest girl in my year and I once heard Florence say I was kind of chubby. So, even though I was chosen, even though I was the perfect fit for Mum and Dad, I don't really match at all.

These days, every time I brush my teeth, I look in the mirror and wonder if my other mother has the same eyes as me. Once, when I was in town, I saw a lady with the same hair and wondered if it was her. I followed her round the supermarket until she got to the frozen-food section, but when she turned round she wasn't a she at all. It was a boy and it gave me such a fright I ran back to the till to find my mum.

Which is sort of funny if you think about it.

I didn't tell Mum though. I'm still not speaking.

This morning, after breakfast, my dad tried to get me to talk again.

31

'What's the capital of Portugal?' he asked and I knew the answer. I like looking at maps or at the enormous globe in the library. I looked up at him, but just as the words were about to come out my mum came into the kitchen with a screwdriver in her hand.

'David, can you give me a hand? I can't quite get the last screw to tighten on Alice's old cot.'

I felt a chill run down my body and a frown appeared on my forehead. Dad looked down at me hopefully.

'Do you want to help too, Alice? We're putting your old cot back together so it'll be ready for your little sister.'

My cot! I wanted to shout. MY COT! Why is she getting my cot? I stood up from the table and left the room, slamming the kitchen door so hard it sort of rattled for ages afterwards.

At dinner time no one said anything about it and I noticed again that Mum wasn't eating anything. She's got this thing where you feel sick all the time. Most mornings I hear her throwing up, but Dad says it's nothing to worry about. He says that pregnant women often get sick, but poor Mum has been sick every morning for months and I'm starting to think it's like my little sister is making her poorly and that can't be a good thing.

At bedtime Mum came to say goodnight. As she kissed my cheek, I wanted to put my arms round her neck and cuddle her, but then she asked me something crazy.

'Do you think you have an old cuddly toy that you'd like to give your new sister? Perhaps it would be nice for you to pick one for her nursery? Or we could go into town and choose one together? Maybe we could get something new for you too?'

I wanted to shove her away. What about the tree house that they'd promised to build for me? Or the trip to the cinema they'd said we'd go on last week? They didn't seem to have time for that any more, but all the time in the world for someone who wasn't even here yet. I wanted to tell her that I didn't want to give my little sister anything. Instead I just turned out the light and rolled over. She sighed and left the room, but as I heard her walk down the wooden hallway I turned the light back on and spied the notebook the doctor lady had given me. There was a blue pen beside it. I still haven't spoken a single word or written one either, but I picked up the pen and looked down at the first blank page. I was going to write something, but then I changed my mind, lay back on the pillow, switched off the light and closed my eyes.

I lay there for quite a long time before I did what I'd been doing a lot; I thought about her. I thought about my other mother. Where was she now? What did she look like? Does she have short chubby fingers like me? Does she like eating peaches straight out of the tin? What does she sound like? What does she do? Some nights I imagine that my other mother is a famous movie star. Some nights I think she's an Olympic gold medallist and nearly always I imagine her trying very hard to find me.

The next morning I woke up, turned on my side and looked at the photograph frame on my bedside table. Me,

Mum and Dad: the three of us smiling together. Then I heard Mum shout up the stairs to tell me to get up, but I didn't. For a while I just lay there, thinking about the blurry black-and-white photograph of my soon-to-be little sister. I wondered if my other mother had been given a picture like that of me and suddenly I had an idea. I sat up quickly, picked up the blue pen, opened up the notebook and on the first clean white sheet I wrote my first words.

I walked into the kitchen slowly and when Mum saw me she turned round and smiled. I looked at her stomach; it was getting bigger now. I held the pad in front of her, but when she saw what I'd written she gasped and put a hand to her mouth. I waited. After a while, she bent down to me and stroked my hair.

'I'll try. I'll do my very best,' she whispered.

One week passed, then two weeks and every time Mum and Dad tried to get me to talk I just picked up the pad and pointed to the words. But nothing happened; they were too busy making my sister's room perfect or buying things for her or visiting the hospital, so I thought they'd forgotten all about my note.

I was wrong.

It was the last day of May and I'd spent all afternoon hiding in the garden with my notebook. I'd started drawing in it. The paper is silky smooth so that my pen glides across the white paper in a way that makes drawing a lot easier than I find at school. That night, when I was getting ready for bed, they came to tell me. They had something for me. A photograph. A photograph of my other mother. There she was, in my dad's hand, between his thumb and forefinger. He held it out towards me.

At first I was scared, more scared than I have ever been in my whole entire life, and as I took the photograph from my father's hands I could see that mine were shaking.

At first I was afraid to look and then I turned the picture over and stared.

6

Alice

When Mum and Dad had left, I stared and stared at the photo. Then I held it right under my bedside light to get a better look. I bent down over the picture to take in every little detail. My other mother was somehow not what I had expected at all.

That night I couldn't sleep. I tossed and turned, and every so often I switched the light on and had another look.

The next day was the same and the day after and the day after that. Her face was all that I could see. Now that I had a picture of her I could put her face into any of the different imaginings that I had. I could see her face when she was a famous ballerina, a princess, an actress, an explorer, an artist, a tennis player winning at Wimbledon. A lot of the time I imagined that she was a nurse. My dad's a doctor and the nurses at the hospital where he works are always so lovely that he calls them the hospital angels. So my favourite thing to imagine is that my other mother is a hospital angel, healing all the sick children in the world. Which is why she can't look after me. It's understandable. I've decided that she's definitely out there at some other hospital and one day she'll come back for me.

Ever since they gave it to me, I've been carrying the photograph everywhere with me and yesterday, when I thought I'd lost it, I got so upset that I cried and cried. I'd only had the thing for a month and already I'd lost her. It was just like the time I lost my favourite rabbit. When I was a little baby, my aunt had given me the softest ever rabbit and I'd called her Rebecca at first, but after a while I just called her Becky Boo. Her fur was sort of silky soft and I used to suck my thumb and hold her against my cheek. I took her with me everywhere.

When I couldn't find the photograph, it was just like the time I left Becky Boo on the train and nobody could find her. Mum bought me another rabbit and even though it was identical it didn't feel the same. It didn't smell the same at all. In the end I just called it Rabbit because I couldn't think of a name and because it didn't really feel like it belonged to me. It didn't feel like it was mine.

As I searched everywhere for the photograph, I felt myself get scared. That was when I realised that I'd not spoken for so long that even if I wanted to talk I might not be able to. It's as though the words won't come out and it kind of frightens me. I stood there, blinking at Mum, with my mouth hanging open and my arms outstretched. I wanted to say: 'I've lost the photograph! I've lost her!' She was so worried she called Dad to come home from the hospital, but by the time he came speeding up the driveway I'd found the photograph in between the pages of my new book and gone back outside to sit under the old cedar tree at the bottom of the garden.

I stared down at her face again, even though by now I'd looked so much that I didn't need the photo to remember her face. Did we look alike? I wasn't sure. She was standing in front of a shop with her hands in her jacket pockets. Where was that shop? I looked closer and I thought I saw something familiar, but I didn't know why. Was it the sign above the shop? Had I seen it before? I closed my eyes to think, but nothing came into my brain and I got distracted when Dad suddenly shouted down to me to say he was going back to work. I watched him waving as he ran up to the driveway. I heard the car as he left and I sat silently looking out to sea.

I looked round the garden and thought of all the secret places I knew. Would I have to show them to my little sister? Culver Manor wouldn't be my place any more. I turned round and looked up at the house. When you drive down the lane to our house, it feels as though there isn't anywhere left to go until you see the black and gold shiny gates and the high white walls that go all round the garden. Dad calls them our 'soft white walls' and says that we're always safe inside them. The thing about our house is that it's the very last house on the coast road and at the very far side of the vale. If you didn't know it was there, you would not know it existed, but everyone in the village knows who I am. I am Dr Richardson's daughter. I am the girl that lives at Culver Manor.

But now I am the girl that won't talk.

What they don't know is that I can't. I have tried. When I'm on my own. I get as far as the first letter and then it stops, and when I try harder it almost hurts. It's like, no matter how hard I try and push the rest of the word out, it won't come. It gets stuck.

Later that week, I was sitting in the rose garden, drawing a butterfly in my notebook, when Mum came outside. She started to cut some of the beautiful pink flowers that smell like honey, and when I got nearer she looked over at me and asked if I was hungry. I was. I was really hungry. My tummy had been rumbling for ages, so I tried as hard as I could to tell her. I thought of the words I wanted to say, and even though I was scared I took a deep breath and opened my mouth But as I did, as I felt the words begin to come up out of my throat, my mum suddenly straightened her back and put both hands on her bulging tummy.

'Oh! She's kicking! David, come quickly!' she shouted.

Dad ran over from the corner of the garden where he'd been weeding; he ran over and bent down so that the side of his face was resting on her stomach. I watched him smile like

I'd never seen him smile before and the words I'd been trying desperately to get out disappeared right back down where they'd been hiding. I spun round and marched inside where I ate all of the strawberries we'd bought earlier at the supermarket, leaving a messy plate and a trail of sticky red fingerprints behind. I stomped upstairs and slammed my bedroom door. My little sister wasn't even here yet and already it felt as though she was taking over. As if she was taking my mum and dad away from me.

After a while, I walked over to the window and looked down at the garden. Mum and Dad were lying side by side on a rug underneath my favourite cedar tree. I watched Mum take her sun hat off so that her long blonde hair fell down in a shimmering golden curtain. I turned and looked in the mirror at my long dark hair. I pulled on one of the curls to get it to straighten, but it just sprang up again. *Stupid curls*, I thought.

The baby will probably have lovely blonde hair like Mum. She'll probably look just like them. She'll have freckles and blue eyes. She'll look just like *them* and be a much better fit than me. I grabbed a hairband and did my best to tie my stupidly thick hair up. I felt myself frowning and that is when I decided to do something I've never done before. The most forbidden thing. No, I didn't go into the library and get my sticky red fingerprints all over Dad's special books. Actually, I thought about it, but I decided it was too nice to stay inside.

When my grandpa was alive, he would say: 'At the bottom of the garden, where the long grass grows, there is a secret door which nobody knows. No one but us knows the door to the shore, where the smugglers came many years before.'

One night, when Florence and her family were staying, we both crept downstairs when we were supposed to be in bed and heard the grown-ups talking all about Culver Cove, so we listened at the door. We heard my dad and my aunt talking about the time, when they were children, they'd snuck out of the house late at night. We listened with amazement as my aunt described a torch-lit scramble down to the shore. Ever since I heard about a moonlit waterfall and pinky white sand, I've wanted to see it for myself, but Mum and Dad would never tell me how to get there. I didn't even know where the path to the shore began. Dad always said it was too dangerous.

Florence and I had held our breath as we heard my dad describe a footpath that was so hidden in places that if you'd never been along it you wouldn't know it was there; he said it was overgrown with purple flowers that cover the shoreline all summer so that if you were a bird, looking down at the hog's back cliffs which drop down to the sea, all you would see is a purple-covered hill. We heard Aunt Aggy describe a little stone seat where the path looks as though it's come to an end, but really you have to duck underneath the last large tree and climb on to a small ledge by the waterfall. 'One slip,' we heard her say, 'and you'll go crashing down on to the rocks.' They had all used the secret path and I didn't even know where it was.

But on that hot day of summer I did several things I wasn't supposed to do. Firstly I ran upstairs to the attic and over to the far corner of the room. Had I seen what I thought I'd seen when I'd been there with Dad? I stood in front of the little door for a few moments as though I was waiting for some little voice to tell me to stop. I felt the cool of the metal handle in my hand and slowly I pushed open the door.

It was exactly how I remembered and, before I had a chance to think, I was standing in front of the faded poster. A picture of a footballer with the words *Mexico 86* in the top right corner and where it was peeling away from the wall I saw the corner of a drawing. My heart beat a little faster and, as I carefully plucked the poster away, flakes of old paint fluttered to the floor. The poster fell forward, clung on to the wall for a moment or two, but then the ancient Blu-Tack gave way and I watched it skid across the floor.

When I looked back up again, I smiled. I *had* been right. It *was* a map and I leaned in closer to get a better look. A perfect map of the house, the garden, and I could just about see the faded outline of a door at the far left corner of the rose garden. Was *that* the door to the shore? A door in the rose garden? I traced the footpath with the tip of my finger as it snaked down the hillside. Culver Cove, a waterfall and the letters A, D, T, J, S and K were written in different colours on the little beach. Aggy? David? Tom? But what were the other letters for? I carefully stuck the poster back on the wall and raced down the stairs. Culver Cove, that's where I was headed, but first I had to find the door.

I went to my room and grabbed my book, my photograph and my drawing pencils and went downstairs. I found my old rucksack, a towel and I stole the lemon cake that Mum had made for the school fair. The cake which I had smelt all morning as it baked in our funny-looking oven; a delicious citrus perfume that had wafted out of the kitchen, down the hall, up the stairs and into my bedroom. I packed my bag, placing the cake inside the towel, and then I crept out of the front door and round the side of the house.

I walked through the rose garden and along the walls where I had played for hours with my friends. I looked carefully up and down all of the faded red bricks and climbed into the flower bed to get closer, bending down and reaching upwards through the climbing roses. The scent of the little yellow buds filled my nostrils and I nearly caught my face on their thorns. Remembering the map, I followed the wall to the far left corner where a large red rose bush stuck out from the wall; its velvety flowers hung down, a pool of scarlet petals at my feet. This had to be the corner where the door was, but I saw nothing but the rose bush.

I turned round and looked back along the walls. Nothing. But, as I climbed down from the flower bed, my foot got caught in a branch and I fell sideways against the wall so that my face was now almost against the warmth of the pale red bricks, and something caught my eye. A shimmer of something, a glimmer of something, a rusted metal bolt. I stood up quickly and, taking my little cardigan off, I wrapped it round my arm to protect it from the thorns.

With a deep breath, I pushed back the rose bush and crawled underneath, and in the darkened corner of the garden, hidden completely by the scented red rose bush, was the door I had been looking for. The secret door which was covered almost completely in ivy. One by one, I peeled back the green tentacles and slowly slid the rusty bolt across and, with a racing heartbeat, I stepped through the door. I stepped through the door to the other side and headed off for the deserted beach where I could leave everything else behind.

But I wouldn't be alone.

7

Zack

When moving day arrived, I felt so sick that I didn't want to eat the toast that Mum had made for me and I ended up feeding my breakfast to a hungry-looking Otter who lay curled up on my feet. Mum was rushing this way and that. The hallway was full of big brown boxes. Boxes filled with what little we had left. I sat there with my head in my hands and my eyes closed. Perhaps something would happen. Perhaps there was time. Maybe some miracle that meant we didn't have to leave after all.

I opened my eyes and looked around at the empty kitchen. I remembered Dad always making me pancakes on Saturdays, and how once he forgot to put the top on the juicer so that pink smoothie sprayed all over the white cupboards, and we both laughed when Mum walked in and a big pink dollop of smoothie dripped down from the ceiling on to her face. Thinking about it made me smile at first, but then it made me feel so sad that I thought for a second I was actually going to cry. My throat got tight and my eyes began to sting, but then Otter farted one of his world-famous stink-bomb farts and I kind of laughed instead.

Mum was upstairs when the doorbell rang so I reluctantly got up, went to the door and opened it.

A fat, red-faced man stood on the step. He wore blue dungarees with the words *A 2 B Removals* in white letters on the chest pocket. He took off his baseball cap to reveal a completely bald head and when he smiled I saw he had a gold tooth.

'Hello! You must be Zacky.'

I frowned. No one calls me Zacky. What an idiot. I turned round and headed back to the kitchen. Not that it stopped him talking.

'I'm Gary. I knew yer dad. Him and me we knew each other when we was teenagers. Jonny and me were like brothers way back when.'

Jonny? My dad was Jonathan, NEVER Jonny. Then Mum appeared and when she saw Gary she ran over and threw her arms round him.

'Oh, Gaz! Thank you so much for this. Thank you so much!'

'Anything for my little Janey,' he said, grabbing a pile of boxes from the hallway and heading back outside.

I looked up at Mum and frowned.

'Don't look at me like that, Zack. Gary is the sweetest man. He used to live in Spain and has only just moved back. He thought the world of your dad. He owns a removal company and he's moving us today for free. Out of the goodness of his heart, so please, BE NICE.'

I felt a bit bad then, so I helped a bit, sort of, and by the time it came to put Otter in the back of the van the whole morning had disappeared. I stood on the road for ages. I looked up and down the street where me and Lou always took our skateboards, where we always had a street party on the last day of summer and where I always used to sit on the pavement, waiting for Dad to come home. I stood like that for ages and, with the heaviest legs and a sort of pain in my chest, I climbed into the van next to Mum.

Gary's van had a radio, but it didn't work so he tried to sing instead and he is the worst singer you ever heard; he even tried whistling a bit, but he kept forgetting the tune and, when we stopped for petrol, I scrambled around in the back of the van for my iPod. I let Otter out and filled up his water bowl so that he could stretch his legs and have a drink. I sat down on a little bench by the van and, when Gary disappeared into the shop, Mum sat down next to me and told me some more bad news. Yeah, I know what you're thinking: as if it could get any worse.

'Zack, I've been wanting to talk to you about Otter. When I start work and you're at school every day, we can't leave

Otter all by himself. It'd be cruel. You know he hates to be all alone. Well, the thing is I discussed it with Hannah and she's going to help us.'

Hannah had visited us loads after Dad died. She's my mum's best friend. They say they're like sisters who just look completely different from each other. Mum is kind of skinny with short hair and Hannah is kind of different. She has big red curly hair just like her daughter Lexi.

'I spoke to Hannah last night and she agrees with me so we're going to let Otter stay with them for a little while . . .'

'What! NO WAY!' I shouted so the whole car park heard. 'No way, Mum! NO WAY! No way is that horrid ginger brat having MY DOG!' I stomped off to grab Otter's collar and knelt down to stroke his ears.

'Zack, firstly Lexi is not a brat.'

I thought about the last time I'd seen her; it wasn't long after the airport incident when Mum took me up to Bristol for the weekend. I was minding my own business, eating a bowl of cereal, when Lexi appeared at the door with her friend Eddie.

'Is it true you kicked a policeman?' Lexi said and I just stared back at her. 'Your mum told my mum that you did.'

Why are girls so annoying? I watched her friend picking a scab on her elbow and I suddenly went off my Shreddies.

'If you want to come for a walk with me and Otter, you're gonna have to be less annoying,' I said, putting my bowl in the sink.

Lexi just laughed and said, 'Well, if you want to come for a walk with *us*, you're going to have to change your top; it's got last-night's dinner down the front of it.'

I shook my head and stroked Otter's ears.

'Look,' Mum said, trying to put her arm round me, 'it's just a temporary thing. I promise. Just until we can get ourselves together. When we've unpacked and settled in, it'll be different. We can come back for Otter. I promise.'

I looked down at Otter's big brown eyes and shook my head. This couldn't be happening. She couldn't do this to me as well.

'Zack, the good news is that Hannah said we can use her spare car, you know, until I can afford one of our own. At least we don't have to walk everywhere now. I know it's not much, but it's a start.'

I refused to talk to her after that and when we arrived outside Hannah's house I wouldn't get out. I saw Hannah and Lexi come running to the van and start making a fuss over MY dog. I watched Otter skip up the driveway as though he knew that his rightful place was in another really big house just like the one we'd left. I sat there for ages, picking the skin around my nails, until Gary told me I had to get out.

'You and your mum are gonna drive down in the car so I'd best get a move on. This old thing isn't as fast as a car.'

I ignored him and stared out of the window.

'Your new home is in one of the most beautiful places in the country. Me and the missus took our caravan there last year; it's magical. You've got woods, moorland with all sort of animals and loads of beaches.'

I was fed up with hearing about how fantastic the place we were going was when I'd just had all my stuff taken off me, my home, my friends, and now my dog was being given away. I got out of the van, slammed the door and slowly went inside. At least, I thought as I wandered into the kitchen, at least there'd be beaches. I remembered the surfing holiday me and Dad had been on in Cornwall and, with a sort of smile, I told myself that maybe there was something to look forward to.

Hannah had made us all a late lunch of a home-made pizza thing which at least tasted good, so I ate four slices. I watched Otter make himself at home and saw how Lexi had already worked out that he likes his ears stroked best. When the time came to go, I felt like I had that morning, like I was in a horrid nightmare that wouldn't stop. As we walked out of the house to the car, Otter came running out of the house and when Mum opened the boot he jumped straight inside. He didn't want to be left behind. He wanted me. He wanted to come with us.

'Look, Mum, see, Otter wants to come, don't you, Ott?'

I was kind of pleased to see that after two and a half years of being my dog Otter wasn't prepared to give up without a fight.

'Look, Mum! Look!' I said to her, but she just shook her head and lifted him out of the boot.

I watched Otter being taken inside. He sat down by Lexi's feet and as we drove away it felt as though my heart would burst.

8

Zack

The rest of the journey took ages and it was on one of those windy roads that make you feel a bit sick. As each mile went on, as we got further and further away from London, I felt myself getting sadder and sadder. I couldn't stop wondering about the new school and what the boys there would be like. What would it be like to go to a school with girls too? Would I make friends? Or would I always be 'the new boy' like Ed who came to my old school, Hardwick Hall, three years ago. I didn't want to be 'the new boy' that didn't know anyone or how to find which classroom I should be in.

I had been at Hardwick for eight years; I knew every room, every corridor, where to sit at break time, which table to sit on at lunch and where the place to hang out was. Now I'd be just like Ed, sitting on my own, getting lost along the corridors, not knowing what to laugh at and what not to laugh at, and being teased for not talking like the rest of us.

I thought of Ed on his first day and how Lou and I had sniggered at his weird American accent, and when me and Lou decided something was funny everyone else joined in. It was ages before that stopped and I know it was kind of mean, but until Ed showed everyone that he was just about the best skateboarder you ever met everyone kind of ignored him. Would that happen to me? Would I be the new kid that everyone teased or ignored until I proved I was cool or something? Then I thought of my dad and it gave me an idea. I'd just tell everyone about him and they'd like me, but Mum had other ideas.

We'd been driving for about an hour when she started to tell me about the new school again.

'You know I told you how your new school is quite a lot different from Hardwick?'

I grunted. Hardwick was a private school and this other place wasn't. Hardwick was boys only; this new place had girls too.

'Somerset Vale is a lot bigger. The students come from all over the area so there'll be quite a mixture of boys and girls.'

'Yeah, Mum, I know. You said, like, six times already.'

'Well, I'm saying again because you haven't been to a school like this before and you haven't been in a classroom with girls and boys from all walks of life. Do you know what I mean by that?'

'I'm not stupid, you know. You've told me already. It'll be different, I get it.'

'I want you to just be careful about what you say when you start. I think it would be a huge mistake to go to this new school telling people about your dad.'

'Why not?' I said angrily, thinking how else I could impress anyone.

'Zack, at your old school having a stuntman dad was cool, but at Somerset Vale the students are the children of farmers and normal people. There won't be anyone there whose parents arrived at school sports day in a helicopter. There won't be anyone who had a chauffeur-driven car to bring them to school or anything like it.'

Why was she telling me this all over again? I wasn't stupid; it wasn't as though I'd lived in some weird rich planet and never left. I met loads of different people when Dad took me with him. I just wish she'd stop going on about the same stuff every day.

'So the thing is, well, put it this way, Zack, if you turn up at your new school and start boasting, if you say things like "my dad was a stuntman", you'll discover, pretty quickly, that no one will like you for it. No one likes a bragger. Just be you and it'll be fine.'

Be myself? What does that even mean anyway? Dad was really cool; why wouldn't I want to speak about him? She kept going on, but I stopped listening to her after a while and instead I tried to see if I could still name every football home ground. I got stuck on Spurs. How could I not remember where Spurs play? It was a road, wasn't it? Gigg Lane? No, that's where Bury play. Spurs play at . . .

'Zack, for God's sake, are you even listening to me?' Mum snapped.

'White Hart Lane. Yes! I knew it!' I blurted out; I knew I couldn't forget where Dad's team played. But Mum just rolled her eyes and sighed.

I must have fallen asleep because when I opened my eyes again Mum had stopped the car at the top of the road. I looked out of the window at the view. Mum saw me staring and smiled.

'This is Porlock Vale, our new home. Amazing, isn't it? It's a long way from London, but it's worth it, right?'

I didn't want to agree, I really didn't. But the land before me was greener than any countryside I had ever seen or at least it was a shade of green that I'd never laid eyes on before. It was lighter, fresher, as though it had just rained, and it stretched out for miles in a sort of patchwork of fields, until I could just make out the blue of the sea. On each side two enormous hills stood as tall as mountains, but dropped into the sea like two giants whose outstretched arms were reaching out to the water.

Mum drove further and further along a twisty road. Then the road became a lane and the lane became a track. We drove higher and higher until I heard my ears pop like they do when you go on an aeroplane. Then she suddenly stopped, got out of the car and told me to follow. I scrambled up a steep bank off the side of the road towards the start of what looked like a path that was covered in rocks and plants that I had never seen before.

'Come on,' she shouted and I had to move quickly to keep up with her.

The path got narrower and narrower. Then it got steeper and steeper, and on either side the funny-looking plants became large thorny bushes which were covered in pretty bright yellow flowers. It got so steep I had to bend down and use my hands to climb up the rocks. I could feel the sweat begin to drip down my back and my breathing become heavier and heavier. My mum, on the other hand, was scrambling up the steep rocky path like a mountain goat, and then she suddenly stopped, stretched out her arms and I watched her take a huge breath.

'Ah, Zack, look at that! I forgot how beautiful Exmoor is. Centre of the universe, that's what my dad used to say.'

And, when I finally climbed up to the spot where she was standing, when I finally reached the top of the hill where Mum stood like some kind of crazy person, I saw with my own eyes a sight I will never forget. It felt as though we were standing right on top of a mountain on the very top of the world, and the valley that I'd seen earlier was below our feet, but this time I could see all of it. The rolling patchwork of fields, the farmhouses, churches and forests, but most of all I could see the sea like it was rising up towards us.

I took a deep breath and smelt not salty sea air, but something different. Something completely unexpected. Coconut. And, as if Mum could read my mind, she put her arm round my shoulders and whispered, 'That's the gorse flower. Some people say it smells like honey, but I don't agree. I think it smells like . . .'

'Coconut,' I said, breathing in the lovely scent once more.

'Yes, like coconut.'

When we got back in the car and set off again, I gazed out of the window at the magnificent view and I started to feel a bit OK. Just a bit. I couldn't remember the last time I'd seen Mum so happy and, for a short while, I forgot all the miserable thoughts and worries. I didn't feel sad or angry or anything like that, but it didn't last very long at all.

We followed the road through the middle of the valley past lots of funny-looking old houses that were all painted a sort of pale yellow colour. We drove through a village and Mum pointed out her old primary school, but, when we turned right to the village of Porlock Weir and towards the sea, all my sort of happy feeling vanished as fast as you can say 'surfboard' because the beaches weren't at all what I had been expecting. They weren't covered in white or yellow sand. They weren't like any beaches I was used to because THERE WAS NO SAND AT ALL. Just rock and stones and some really big boulders.

Mum had told me over and over how amazing the beaches were and I'd thought I could go bodyboarding like we'd done on holiday. It was the one thing I'd thought might just be OK, but, as we drove down to the harbour, I saw with horror that all three beaches were full of stones. Massive stones. The sort of stones that break bones. And when I saw the sign 'Danger! No swimming' I felt my blood boil and the little angry feeling became one enormous shouting rage.

'You lied! You totally lied to me! You said there were beaches! Proper beaches. You can't even swim here,' I yelled, pointing at the sign.

Mum stopped the car outside a row of white cottages and sighed.

'Zack, these are beaches. We can go rock pooling and . . .'

'Rock pooling? Are you mental? I'm not five years old, you know!'

This was the moment that Mum lost her temper with me, and she took her seat belt off and banged her tiny fists on the steering wheel.

'Zachery Drake! I know you're not five years old, but right now I wish you bloody well were. Because then you were sweet and adorable and not a spoilt, grumpy brat.'

'Well,' I said, shouting back, 'I'm so sorry, Mother, sorry for being born, sorry for being such a horrible *accident* after all!'

And with that I got out of the car, slammed the door and ran as fast as I could out of the harbour, along the stupid, stony beach, and I decided that today was probably the worst day of my entire life.

9

Alice

Remembering every little detail I had overheard, I set off down the overgrown footpath. I walked carefully and close to the left, watching out for the edge and making sure I held on to branches in places where I thought I might slip. I felt my heart beat a little faster with each step that I took, but it was a kind of exciting feeling too. The path was so overgrown that the green branches made it feel a bit like I was walking through a tunnel.

I followed the path until I got to the stone seat; the words *Culver Cove* were carved into it. My legs were feeling tired so I sat down for a while and watched the sea below. The waters were calm and blue, and I could just make out the large rocks where the smugglers used to bring their boats filled with treasure. When I climbed underneath a tree, I had to push the branches away from my face with the back of my hand.

As I crawled through the darkness, I felt my heart beat quickly and for a moment I wondered if I should go back, but as the thought entered my head I caught sight of the waterfall. Its crystal waters cascaded down the hill in a loud rushing sound and I made the mistake of following the water with my eyes. As I watched the water descending, I felt myself get dizzy and my foot almost slipped off the edge. I grabbed hold of the rocks and tried to catch my breath again. I moved forward towards the ledge. Now I had to do the hard part and jump over the edge to the other side.

I looked once more at the rushing water and told myself not to look down. I held my head high and concentrated on the large rock face in front of me, counting one, two, three. But I didn't move. One. Two. Three. Again I stayed rooted to the spot. Could I reach it? I placed one foot forward and tried to measure the gap. Would I make it? Had I ever jumped that far? Should I just turn round and run back home? *Home*, I thought, remembering my mum and dad in the garden and the stupid baby kicking. They didn't need me any more. So I took a deep breath and, thinking about the pretty beach which lay ahead of me, I jumped.

It happened like slow motion. My body tipped forward and my feet sprang into the air. I saw the other side getting closer, closer, a gentle breeze on my face as I descended, but, just as my toes were almost touching the ledge, I felt the ruck-sack on my shoulder suddenly being tugged violently backwards and I had just enough time to pull my arm free of the strap. I landed hard, falling forward on to my hands and knees, and I watched in horror as my bag tumbled down the rock face all the way to the shore.

I wiped the sweat from my forehead and listened to the sound of the waterfall above me. I could just about see the water through the thick branches and I knew I had to be close. Finally I spied the little stone steps; I bent down to climb under the last branch and crawled out from the darkened footpath into the bright light of the sunshine.

At first I felt as though I'd walked right into a painting or on to one of those secret islands where ancient tribes still live. It couldn't be real. It didn't feel real. The sand wasn't yellow, it was pinkish white. The sea wasn't grey or blue, it was turquoise, and the two rocks on each side of the cove stood proudly like pillars. Like the gateway to another world. And it was hot. Stinking hot. I looked back up the steep hill and wondered why Dad had told me the path was covered with rocks. Why had he always said it was impossible to get down to Culver Cove? Why had he lied?

I took off my shoes and walked barefoot on the warm sand. A seagull flew above my head and I watched it circle lower and lower; I watched it swoop and dive. Then I saw him. Sitting bare-chested and cross-legged on our beach was a boy I'd never seen before. I quickly ducked behind a large rock. Who was he? What was he doing on our beach?

I peeped out to look again. He had my bag! I got really angry when he began to open it. My hands clenched into fists when he started looking through it. I saw him pull out the towel and watched in horror as the lemon cake rolled on to the beach where it became covered in sand. I marched out from my hiding place and strode right up to him. I wanted to yell, but I still couldn't make a sound, and suddenly I found myself standing right over him. The boy jumped up quickly, dropped my bag and, as he looked down at me, I saw his face in the soft light of the sun.

His hair was thick and darkest brown, and now that I was closer I could see that it was soaking wet. His eyes blinked in the light and it was only when he held up a hand to shield his eyes that I realised that he was like no one I had ever seen before. His eyes looked as though someone had used a big black felt tip to draw round the coloured bit. It made the blue look like wet paint and the angry feeling sort of melted away. I just stared. Then I felt myself blushing from my chest right up to the hairs on the back of my neck. He looked at me with squinty eyes and then he smiled in a way that made me feel as though he was really happy to see me. In a way that made me think he knew me, that he wasn't really a stranger after all.

We stood like that silently for what seemed like forever and then he turned round and left. Just like that. I watched him as he climbed along the rocks and disappeared back round the headland to the village.

Who was he?

I sat on the beach until my face was burning from the sun and, as there was nowhere shady to sit, I felt hot and uncomfortable. After a while, I pulled out the photograph of my other mother and stared down at her face. Did she like beaches? Did she like to swim?

I was so hot and worried about getting back before it was dark on my way home, that strangely it wasn't so bad the second time around. As I slid the rusty bolt back across the door to the garden, I knew I wanted to go back to the beach again. As I climbed out from underneath the red rose bush, I turned and shook my head. You just wouldn't know the door was there and, as I kicked the red petals back into place, I realised that it looked exactly as I had found it.

I tried to sneak back into the house, but Mum and Dad were waiting for me and they were really angry. I stood in the kitchen and stared at the floor.

'Alice, I am so disappointed in you,' Mum said, shaking her head. 'I love you so much, but you really can't do that sort of thing.'

I nodded and waited to hear what my punishment would be. Going to the beach was forbidden. It was the golden rule, never to be broken, and I waited nervously.

'Alice, what are we going to do?' Mum sighed.

I held my breath.

'Does your mum have to lock the door and hide the key?' Dad said.

I thought about the rusty bolt on the door.

'Alice, that cake was for the stall. I made that for the school fair so that they can raise money for the new school bus.'

The cake? I'd forgotten all about it. It had probably been carried off by a seagull. They were mad about the cake? They didn't know where I'd been and I was so relieved that I almost smiled and said something, but then I thought of the boy on the beach and the words got stuck. I tried to look as sorry as I could, but Mum and Dad just shook their heads.

'I'm going to have to make another one now. I haven't got time to make you dinner as well. You and your dad can go into the village and get something there.'

Mum gave my dad a funny look and then I spied the little pad next to the phone and, without thinking, I wrote: *I am sorry*.

Mum smiled, kissed my cheek and whispered in my ear, 'I guess I do make the best cakes, eh?'

10

Zack

As I ran down the road and away from Mum, I felt like I wanted to shout in my loudest ever voice, 'I just don't want to be here!' Why didn't she get it? Why couldn't we have just stayed somewhere I knew or somewhere that at least had real beaches and not these stupid, stony, 'Danger no swimming' beaches? What's the point of that?

I heard her calling after me, but I kept on running down the footpath until I couldn't hear her any more. When I got to the end of the lane, I saw Gary and the removal van parked outside the row of cottages I sort of remembered from that photo Mum tried to show me. He waved at me to come over, but I turned away and jumped over the harbour wall on to the stupid, stony beach. I kicked a few stones, but that kind of hurt, and in the end I went to the far side of the so-called beach, sat on a boulder and tried to throw pebbles into the water. The tide was pretty far out and the greyish stones just clattered down to the beach without reaching the sea.

I looked back to the harbour and could just make out the side of the last white cottage. I could see Gary again and, when he started heading my way, I got up and left. The stones got bigger and bigger until I was just clambering over bigger and bigger rocks and there wasn't really any beach left, just a green headland which disappeared to the left. I turned my head and looked upwards at the hill; it was almost vertical, but it was covered in purple flowers, and then I saw something which made my heart sink: 'Private property. Keep out.' I looked at the rusting sign which was hanging off a chain and thought that, if I hadn't turned my head, I wouldn't have seen the sign so I pretended I hadn't and carried on anyway.

It must have been after four o'clock, but it still felt really warm, and as I scrambled towards the last boulder I felt really hot and hungry. Mum says I'm always hungry these days and I think she might be right, not that constantly eating has made me grow taller or anything because I used to be one of the shortest boys in my class.

I took off my hoody, wrapped it round my waist and climbed like a monkey on to the last grey boulder which was at least twice as tall as me. I had to slot my fingers into the grooves on the rock face just like my dad had shown me when we were in France. 'Always keep three points of contact,' he'd said. Just before the top I saw that there were no more little ledges or holes to put my hands into. I felt my heart beating quickly and, even though I could almost hear my dad's voice in my head, it didn't stop me from feeling afraid. I just wasn't like him at all. Dad would just get on and do stuff without being scared, but I'd never be as brave as him. I had to heave my entire body on to the top of the rock and it left me panting and sweating so hard I had to lie down, close my eyes and rest for a bit. But when I opened them again and turned round I saw what lay hidden on the other side of the headland.

I blinked and rubbed my eyes to make sure it wasn't some kind of crazy mirage and, when I realised it wasn't that or a dream, I grinned from ear to ear. Hiding, tucked away from view, was a beach. A real beach! A proper sandy beach at last and I almost jumped down to the other side. Well, I would have jumped, but it was pretty high up so I kind of slid on my bottom until I felt the warm sand between my toes. It was almost like the beach me and Dad had sailed out to on our last holiday. And, as I looked up towards the other side, I saw it had something which made it probably the most amazing beach I had ever seen. It had a waterfall. It came sort of crashing down from the top of the hill to the sand. I shielded my eyes from the glare of the sun and I couldn't be sure, but I swear I saw something moving in the green bushes just above me. I waited for a while then I decided that I must have imagined it.

I walked along the sandy cove towards where the waterfall came down the hillside. The sand was a soft sort of pale pink and when I looked down I saw there were millions of tiny pink and white bits of shell that sort of sparkled in the sunlight. The water on the shoreline was shallow and warm, and the large grey rocks that jutted out of the water created a lagoon like I had only ever seen in movies. As I got nearer to the waterfall, the rushing sound of water was almost deafening and I held my hand under the water. Cold. *Freezing* cold, but I took a deep breath and dipped my head under the icy rush of it. It felt amazing and my whole body cooled down so that I felt comfortable again. I turned back and saw the sun was dipping lower in the sky. I knew I wouldn't have long before Mum or Gary came to find me; besides, I was so hungry that I would have to head back at some point. But, for now, I didn't want to leave.

I sat down at the far side of the little cove and rested my back against the warmth of the rocks and looked around at the secret, hidden beach. My tummy rumbled again. Then something else rumbled and, when I turned to look, I had just enough time to dive out of the way before it hit me straight on the side of the head. At first I thought it was an enormous rock and it scared the pants off me. I thought, *Oh no, I'm going to be squashed to death*, and, as I rolled out of the way, my heart was pounding quickly. But when I sat up again and saw what the mysterious flying object was I realised I needn't have been scared at all, not unless a flying Barbie rucksack can kill you. It made me laugh and I placed it to one side where its little Barbie girl owner could find it.

After a while, I thought I could smell something lovely and lemony, and when I leaned in towards the bag I realised that it was coming from inside. My stomach rumbled once more so, after I had glanced around to check if there was anyone else about, I picked up the bag and unbuckled the clasp. The smell of lemons got stronger and I would have bet my guitar, my keyboard and my iPod that there was some kind of cake hiding in Barbie world. I pulled out a pale blue towel and watched in horror as the predicted cake rolled out of it and down the sandy beach.

The girl must have moved like a ghost or something because I didn't hear her creep up on me at all. The next thing I knew there she was, standing over me, and she gave me such a fright that I jumped up and dropped the bag. She was a lot smaller than me and I thought that she reminded me of someone I knew, but I couldn't think who. At first I thought she was going to shout because her mouth hung open, but she didn't. I panicked as I remembered the 'Private property. Keep out' sign. I held my hand up to shield my eyes and to look out for some kind of grown-up who was sure to come marching over any minute and tell me to get off the private beach. I suddenly felt scared, but then I remembered what Mum often said to me: 'Zack, when in doubt, just smile because no one can stay mad at you for long. You'll break all the girls' hearts with that smile of yours.'

So that is what I did. Sounds dumb, doesn't it? Sounds well stupid, but when I smiled at the girl she stopped looking so angry. She didn't shout. She didn't say one thing. Not one single word. She just stared and stared. She went red so I think she was either blushing or she had sunburn all of a sudden, but still she did not say one word. I was sure that her mum or dad would appear any minute and so I turned round and ran away.

It took me ages to climb back along the rocks and it seemed loads harder than on the way in. When I finally got back to where Gary's van was parked outside the middle white cottage, Mum was so mad at me that everything she said was a sort of shouty bark. Gary didn't say much to me at all, he just went back and forth with the rest of the boxes, but Mum went on and on at me for ages. She went on and on at me until I was shouting back at her and everyone that was in the harbour was staring, and when I finally went inside and slammed the door I saw our new home for the very first time.

11

Alice

Dad and I got in his car and drove up the long winding driveway to the road. He didn't say anything at first, but when we turned on to the lane he did this thing where he sort of pinches your knee and it tickles so much I actually laughed really, really loudly.

'That's better, Alice. It would be a shame if I never got to hear your laughter again.'

We drove down the winding lane towards the village and now that all the oak trees had their leaves the road looked a bit dark. We turned left at the churchyard and down the hill past the post office where Pippa lives, and Dad parked up by the bookshop so we could walk down the lane towards the harbour. We ordered fish and chips from the Boathouse Café and the two of us sat down on the harbour wall and ate delicious, hot, salty chips. There were quite a few big boats to look at and, as I waved at a man who was lowering the anchor on his little sailing boat, we heard really loud shouting. Dad and I turned to look. Actually, everyone turned to look.

At the end of the harbour wall is a little bridge that you have to cross to get to the beach and a row of three white cottages. Years ago, they were the cottages that the fishermen used to live in, but these days they're the sort of cottages that people stay in for their holidays. The middle one is bigger than the other two and it has a pretty front garden with roses that climb up the front and round the doorway.

Parked on the narrow cobbled lane was a blue van with the words: A 2 B Removals. *No job too big or small.*

The shouting began again and a woman emerged from inside the van, carrying two large boxes. We watched her carry her heavy load into the cottage, but when she appeared again my dad suddenly sat up and craned his neck.

'I don't believe it!' he said, shaking his head. 'I think that's . . .' But he suddenly stopped talking and rubbed the back of his head, and when I looked up at him he seemed kind of sad. 'When I was younger, I used to be friends with the girl that lived there. My brother, Aunt Aggy and I used to have a lot of fun together.' The way he said 'used to' made it sound miserable.

I watched him gaze out to sea for a while. Mum once told me that, after my dad's older brother died, Grandma got very sick, but she didn't have an illness that made your body hurt, she had an illness that made her feel very sad all of the time and she spent most of it in bed with the curtains drawn. I thought about Uncle Tom. Even though there are lots of photographs of him in our house, my dad hardly ever talks about him. There's a garden bench at the back of our house with his name on and sometimes I see Dad sitting there with a book, but he never seems to turn the pages.

'Your mum made Culver Manor beautiful again,' Dad said, looking down at me. 'She made the gardens so lovely and the house full of light and colour, and now I wouldn't ever want to live anywhere else. You brought the laughter and the happiness back, but it didn't used to be like that.'

I looked up at him and because I didn't want him to look upset any more I leaned into him and squeezed him tightly.

'Anyway,' he said, trying to look cheerful again, 'we all spent a lot of time down here at the coastguard cottages and Jane Rowe was the girl who lived in the middle house. She was quite a tomboy. She wasn't afraid of anything and she didn't mind telling you what to do either.' He laughed and shook his head.

At that moment the shouting started again and we watched Jane Rowe appear from inside the blue van again.

'All I asked you to do was help,' she barked. 'I've had to do nearly everything by myself! Where the hell have you been? Gary has been looking all over for you. I thought you'd had an accident.'

And a voice shouted back from inside the van, 'Well, I thought I was the accident, MOTHER.'

Everyone was staring and some people were whispering to each other too. I looked up at my dad. He raised an eyebrow and whispered, 'Ooh, nothing like new people to get everyone talking, eh?'

He looked at me hopefully, but I just frowned and thought, *Couldn't even if I wanted to.*

Then the voice from inside the van appeared. A boy. He had his back to us and was carrying a large lamp in one hand and a kettle in the other. He stopped just in front of the house and this time he shouted not just so the harbour could hear, but the whole of the vale too.

'I didn't ask to be born, you know!'

I thought that was going to be the end of it, but a tiny upstairs window opened and the woman stuck her head out.

'Zachariah Ethan Drake, if I had known you'd be a selfish, spoilt little brat, I can tell you now, young man, if you had asked to be born, I WOULD HAVE SAID NO!' she yelled.

I gasped, but my dad sort of laughed. I had never, ever seen people shout at each other like that. Not ever, and I know I shouldn't say so, but it was kind of fun to watch. I think that every single person in the harbour was waiting to see what happened next. I almost held my breath and, as if he could sense us all staring, the boy suddenly turned round.

'WHAT ARE YOU ALL STARING AT?' And, with that, he went inside and slammed the front door. It was difficult to see his face, but I could swear it looked like the boy on the beach. If it was him, what did he mean when he said he was the *accident*? How could a person be an accident?

'Oh dear,' said Dad. 'He looks like trouble.'

And, as we drove home, I thought of the letters that I'd seen on the map. Was Jane the J?

12

Alice

Today is the first day of the summer holidays and guess what? It's raining. I haven't been down to Culver since my secret excursion, but we're going on holiday at the weekend. Well, we're going up to Scotland for a week to see Aunt Agatha, Uncle Alistair and my cousins Florence and Casper.

Florence and I get on like best friends, even though she's over a year older than me, but Casper is just about the most annoying little toad you ever met. He's seven years old and the last time he came to visit us at Culver Manor he locked himself in the playroom and wrote on the walls. Every night he had a massive tantrum about going to bed so that Aunt Aggy had to chase him all over the house, up and down the hallway, until he hid behind one of the red velvet curtains and when she tried to drag him away he held on to the curtains and pulled them down.

The thing about Casper is, apart from his whiny, screaming, whingy voice, apart from his horrid, pasty white face that gets redder and redder when he has a tantrum, apart from all of that, he's a telltale. And he makes stuff up, like, all the time. He once gave himself a Chinese burn and blamed it on me. He once said I'd pushed him off the sofa and Mum actually believed him so I got sent out of the television room. One day he slapped himself across the face, smiled at Florence and burst into tears. Florence and I watched in horror as he ran down the hallway shouting: 'Mummy! Mummy! Florence slapped me!'

'I'm telling Mummy,' he'll say if he sees me and Florence doing anything out of the ordinary. 'I'm telling Mummy on you and then you'll be sorry.'

And guess what? If we don't get told off like Casper had hoped then he really loses it. Last time it happened he actually kicked, spat and swore at all the grown-ups. In the end Uncle Alistair, who is bigger and broader than any man you have ever seen (when I was little I thought Uncle Alistair really was the giant from *Jack and the Beanstalk*), picked Casper up, tucked him under his arm and carried him straight up to bed – it was the middle of the day. Florence and I had found it really hard not to laugh as we watched Casper being carried upstairs like a parcel, but I bet the grown-ups just thought, 'Thank goodness.' I actually think that everyone is much, much happier when he's not around.

I'm not making it up; he really is THAT BAD.

Problem is we're going to his house and Mum says that me not talking at all might be a bit of a problem with Casper, especially when he's in his own kingdom or at least his own castle. And guess what? Casper really does live in a castle. Aunt Agatha is my dad's sister and she married Lord Pengarden of Pengarden Castle. So when Caspar sings: 'I'm the king of the castle and you're the dirty rascal!' it's completely true. Although he's the horrid little 'King Brat Rascal' as Florence calls him.

We packed the car and set off at five o'clock in the morning when it was still dark because it takes all day to get there. Last time we went I slept most of the way and this time, with Mum being really pregnant, she wanted to have space to spread out on the back seats, so I got to sit in the front instead. I love Dad's car; it's one of those high-up truck-type cars that you can take off–road, and Dad had promised me and Florence that he'll take us out of the castle grounds and over to the glen.

On the way up Dad came up with a plan. He said that, so everyone would understand, perhaps we could say I had lost my voice instead and, seeing as Dad's a doctor, they'd believe him. But, as soon as we arrived and Dad told them, I could tell from Aunt Aggy's face that she and Uncle Alistair knew that wasn't true. But at least it meant that toady-faced Casper wouldn't be more of a toad than he already is.

The first thing I noticed was that Florence had changed a great deal since last Christmas when they came to stay at our house. Florence looks just like the rest of the Richardson family: fair, tall and skinny. But the last time I saw her she had braces and she still liked to play the sort of games that I do. We were still sort of best friends and we loved to stay up late in her bedroom at the top of the castle's east tower.

This time it was different. Florence was even taller and she no longer had braces. She was wearing make-up too, and spent the whole time checking her mobile phone and was always on Facebook. In the end it seemed to me that it didn't matter that I wasn't talking because Florence didn't want to talk to me much at all and, when Dad said we could go off-road in the car, she just rolled her eyes and said she didn't want to. She was really interested in Mum and her enormous pregnant tummy though, and even wanted to feel it when the baby was kicking again which I thought was just stupid, stupid, stupid.

So Florence didn't spend much time with me and we never stayed up late together, not even once. Casper was the exact same horrid, pain-in-the-neck, pasty-faced toad I remembered from Christmas time. I saw him pull the cat's tail, kick the dog on purpose and, when Aunt Aggy told him he had to eat his vegetables or he wouldn't grow big and strong like the rest of us, he just pointed at me and said: 'Alice always eats her greens and she's *still* really small!'

It's true, I am small. I looked round the table. I looked at the 'real' family, at how alike they were and how I am nothing like them at all. I thought of my soon-to-be-born little sister and how she'd probably look just like them all too. I felt like an alien or at least a cuckoo. As I looked round the table of pale, freckly faces, I felt the tears trickle down my cheeks so I pushed my chair away from the table and slowly walked out of the kitchen. Maybe I was the one everyone would be happier without.

I wandered down the castle hallway, past the suits of armour and the tapestries that hang down from the walls. I felt the cool of the stone floor on my bare feet and it seemed to me that the corridor just got longer and longer. As I climbed the stone stairs to the west tower, it felt as though there were more steps than there had been before, as though I'd never reach the top, and when I finally got to my bedroom I closed the door behind me softly.

I sat down on the bed and pulled out my book, turning to the back where I'd put the photograph of my other mother. I stared and stared at her and didn't stop crying until I felt arms round my shoulders. I didn't stop when she kissed my forehead and tried to hold me close, and at first I laughed because Mum's bump is so big now that she couldn't really cuddle me properly; it sort of got in the way. Then I stopped laughing and a frown began to grow deeper and deeper across my face until I felt a little angry feeling begin to twist inside my tummy. My stupid sister was already coming between us.

'Alice,' Mum said slowly. 'Do you think you might like to talk a little bit? Just try a little for me, would you do that?'

I shook my head.

'Can I tell you a secret?' she said, stroking my hair, and I nodded. 'Your dad was about four years old when Aunt Aggy was born and, when she was a tiny baby, do you know what he said to Grandma and Grandpa?' I shook my head and waited. I loved hearing about what my mum and dad were like when they were little, especially if they were naughty. 'Well, your dad got a bit cross and he marched into the kitchen, looked over at his little sister and said, "Can we take her back now?"'

I laughed.

'And now your dad and Aggy are like best friends, aren't they?'

She was right, but I couldn't imagine that I'd want to be best friends with the new baby.

'You're going to be a brilliant big sister, Alice, I just know it. Are there any names you like?'

I shrugged.

'Would you like to help me and Dad choose a name?'

I shrugged again.

'Maybe you could try just saying the first letter?'

I wanted to tell her there and then. I wanted to tell her how I had tried really hard, but the words kept getting stuck, and now every time I wanted to talk I got so scared that it felt as though my throat was being squeezed tightly. But I didn't say anything and that night, our last night at Pengarden Castle, I slept beside my mum and my soon-to-be little sister, and I prayed that she wouldn't be anything like horrid, toad-faced Casper.

Nothing could be worse than a screaming pale pink brat who took over, changed everything and made my life much worse.

When our week away came to an end, I was so glad to be going home. Aunt Aggy's cook made us the most delicious car picnic that I had ever eaten. Smoked salmon, roast beef and chicken sandwiches on the fluffiest, softest white bread, but Mum didn't want any of it. She wasn't feeling sick or anything like that; she had her very own very weird picnic. She'd been eating some strange things lately and Dad said that sometimes pregnant women have these cravings for a particular food and, no matter how disgusting it sounds, it tastes really amazing to them. So, while Dad and I tucked into our normal picnic, she was eating a peanut butter, beetroot and ketchup sandwich and my mum NEVER eats ketchup. When Dad and I had the lovely slices of rich fruit cake, Mum ate Cheesy Wotsits dipped in strawberry yoghurt which almost made me feel sick.

We had to stop the car six times so that Mum could go to the toilet. Somewhere between Birmingham and Bristol, somewhere between this life and the next, I watched my mum waddle like a duck back to the car. It made me realise just how large her bump was and I thought about my other mother again. What was she like when she was pregnant with me? Did she have to eat lots of crazy foods? Did she get hot one minute and cold the next? Did she burst into tears because her favourite jumper wouldn't fit? Did she get really cross because her feet had swollen up so much all her shoes were too tight? Did she fart ALL THE TIME? Did I kick her tummy as much as my soon-to-be little sister? Did she have someone like my dad to look after her?

It made me feel sad again. It made me wonder all the bad wonderings. Like, if my mum is going to love my soon-to-be little sister like she loves me, why couldn't my other mother love me like that too?

Why was I adopted?

I thought about it all the way home so, when we got back to Culver Manor, I went up to my bedroom and took out the photograph. I sat down on my bed and stared once more. I held the photograph up to my face to see if there was anything I'd missed, any little clue that might tell me more than I could see, but there was nothing; it was just a photo of a beautiful girl with long black hair standing outside some shop that could be anywhere.

I wanted to sleep, but I kept turning the questions over and over and over again. It felt as though I wouldn't ever sleep again until I knew the answers, but how could I find out if I couldn't talk? How could I ask if I was too scared to speak? And now I had even *more* questions that I wanted the answers to it was like my head was bursting with mysteries I might never solve. So I got up, switched the light on, grabbed the notebook and, turning to a clean white page, I wrote a list.

Questions I want the answers to

Why was I adopted?

Where is my other mother now?

When my little sister is born, will we still have a family birthday and will she get presents too?

Why did Mum and Dad lie about the footpath to Culver Cove?

Why does Dad never talk about his brother Tom?

What do the letters on the map all stand for?

Who is the boy in the cottage and why is he an accident?

Will Dad build the tree house like he promised?

I drew a few little doodles too and when I heard footsteps on the hallway I quickly switched off the light and climbed back into bed.

I still couldn't fall asleep, so I lay awake, listening to the owls hooting in the woods behind the house. I listened to the waves crashing on the shore and I decided there and then that tomorrow I'd go to the beach once more.

13

Zack

If I said our new cottage was half the size of our old house, I'd be telling a massive lie. It wasn't half the size or even a quarter either. It was so small that you could fit the entire downstairs of the cottage into our old kitchen and there'd still be room for a car. The upstairs was a bit bigger, but there was only one bathroom and a shower that had a slow, drip-like trickle that meant washing one leg would take about a week. My room wasn't so bad. It was just big enough for the double bed that Hannah had given us and, when I lay down on it, I could just look out of the window and see the sea.

After our big argument outside with everyone staring at us, I'd flopped down on my bed and lay there for ages. Then Mum knocked softly on the door and came in.

'Zack, I'm sorry. I know this is a lot to take in. I know you're mad at me, but if I'd told you that the beaches were not really good for bodyboarding, it would have made you even madder. There is another beach though.'

I immediately thought about the little cove I'd found, but Mum didn't mean that one.

'I'll take you on Monday if the weather stays like this. Woolacombe is about an hour's drive away and that really is a surfers' paradise.'

'Isn't there one I could maybe just walk to?'

Mum looked at me funnily. 'No,' she said, looking worried. 'Well, there is a beach just round the headland, but you can only reach it at low tide and it's private. Do you know what that means, Zack? It means you do not ever go there. Ever.' She pointed at me seriously. 'Ever!' she said even louder.

'How come?'

'Because . . . when I was younger . . .' She paused, turning her wedding ring round and round. 'When I was a bit younger than you, we . . .' She stopped suddenly again and looked down at the floor, bit her bottom lip and rubbed the corner of her jumper as though she was trying to get rid of an imaginary stain. I waited, but she didn't say anything more. She turned and left the room quickly, but came back a minute later with a large map.

'I got this for you. You like maps, don't you?' I nodded and she unfolded the map and laid it out on the bed. 'Look, here's Porlock Weir. That is where we are, that's the village

86

and the road into town. That's where I stopped the car and the hill we walked up.'

I read the words 'Porlock Hill'. My eyes scanned the map down across the vale to the sea. I liked that I could see all the places I'd seen from the hill. I read all the names until I got to the headland at the far side of the beach. The place I'd been. The secret, hidden beach.

'Culver Cove,' I read and Mum nodded, but when I looked up at her she seemed kind of sad or something.

I traced my finger along the map where I'd seen the waterfall and when I stopped at a square symbol Mum turned to me.

'That's Culver Manor. Culver Cove belongs to that big house and you can only get there by the path above it or when the tide is really low and Zack,' she said, looking at me very seriously, 'you mustn't ever go there.'

She didn't say anything for a while, but I watched her turn and look through the window and out to sea. She sat like that for ages and when she spoke again it was in a voice I hadn't ever heard before, like it didn't really belong to her at all.

'There's a very, very dangerous current just there,' she said, turning back to the map and pointing to the spot where I'd climbed up on to the massive rock. 'I know you're a strong swimmer, but that undercurrent is dangerous. You can't see it, you can barely feel it and before you know it you're being dragged out here,' she said, pointing to the other side of the bay, 'where you'll be smashed against the rocks.'

'OK, OK, Mum, I get it. I promise.'

Mum leaned forward and kissed the top of my head.

'Now, how about we get ourselves some fish and chips?'

I grinned at her and the two us left the cottage, crossed the little stone bridge and headed out towards the glorious vinegary smell that filled the street.

14

Zack

The next day me and Mum had an extra-long lie-in. Actually, I can easily stay in bed until lunchtime, but Mum said we had to try and do all the unpacking which, on a scale of one to ten of total boringness (ten being picking my toenails), was about a fifteen. And even though we didn't have much stuff, and even though the cottage is really small, it took us ages to get everything unpacked. Even then stuff still seemed to be missing because two days later I still couldn't find the earphones for my iPod.

'Let's go into town then, Zack. It'll give me a chance to show you around,' Mum said.

I didn't really want to be shown around. I didn't care what the town looked like. I was like 678 per cent not interested. I rolled my eyes at her and turned back to the television.

'Zack, don't be like that. You'll need to be able to find your way around.'

I turned up the volume on the TV, but Mum didn't like that very much.

'Up! Now! Go on! Get your backside upstairs and get dressed into something that hasn't been on your bedroom floor for two days!' I stared up at her. She glared down at me. 'Do you want new earphones or what?' I legged it upstairs.

'And by the way,' she said, shouting after me, 'a wet towel will not dry if it's left in a heap on the floor!'

We drove back along the valley road away from the sea and through the tiny villages that were scattered up and down the valley, turning right at the blue sign to Minehead.

We parked up and Mum showed me the main street and where to get the bus from.

'Nothing's changed, you know,' she said, looking into the window of an old café. 'I used to come here when I was your age.'

I peered inside and saw nothing out of the ordinary. Just a plain old café like ones I'd seen a million times.

'Come on,' she said, 'let's get something to eat.'

It didn't look very exciting, but I was hungry and I'd noticed the blackboard had the words 'World's Greatest Pasty' written in large white letters.

We sat down at a table by the window which had one of those ketchup bottles shaped like a tomato and, as I stared out across the street, I thought about the café near our old house. It had those ketchup bottles too, but sometimes they got all gummed up with dried sauce and you couldn't get the ketchup out.

Dad took me there for breakfast one morning and instead of waiting for the waitress to ungunk the sticky plastic bottle I had kind of squeezed and squeezed until a fountain of red sauce came bursting out of the lid. It squirted out with such force that it sprayed ketchup all over me, Dad and the table next to us. And, when I looked up at Dad's ketchup-splattered shirt, he'd grabbed a fork and held it to his red chest. '*Argh!*' he cried. 'But I had so much life to live.' It made me laugh out loud. It was a line from our favourite movie. It was a zombie movie that I really wasn't supposed to watch because it was rated fifteen, but Dad let me watch it anyway. Mum didn't know: it was our little secret.

'Zack? Zack? You still with me?'

I looked back at Mum. 'If Dad hadn't died, if he hadn't been in that plane, do you think he would have lived as long as Granddad?' I don't know why I said it, but somehow it seemed unfair that Dad died so young and some people get to be so old.

Mum suddenly looked sad. I knew the look. It was usually followed by crying, and I quickly grabbed a napkin and held it out to her.

'Oh, Zack,' she said, wiping a tear from her cheek. 'Oh, my beautiful boy, I don't know.' I watched her do that weird gulping thing she does when she's trying to stop herself from crying and I quickly looked around to see if anyone was looking. I hate it when she cries. I was going to get up and sit next to her, but then I spied someone on another table get their food.

'I hope my pasty will be as big as that.' And it was.

On the way home Mum made a quick detour so she could show me my new school. She stopped the car at the entrance. I peered out of the window through the big metal gates and my stomach flipped over. It was huge and very modern-looking, but I could see from where I was sitting that the paint was peeling off the gates and they looked rusty and uncared for.

'So what do you think?' Mum said cheerily.

What did I think? What I thought was, *Oh no, please don't make me go there*. What I thought was, *Please just let me go back to Hardwick with my friends*.

She saw me looking miserable and then she said something weird. 'If it was good enough for me, it'll be good enough for you.' I looked back at the fading school sign and my heart sank deeper and deeper.

The next week we didn't get to go to the surfing beach because Mum had to keep going for job interviews and I just spent a lot of time sitting in the car, waiting. 'We'll go tomorrow,' she kept saying, but then there was another interview or it rained, and by the time we had a perfect sunny day it was August 5th and Mum ruined it all anyway.

'Zack!' she shouted up the stairs. 'Zack, I got the job. I got the job!'

We had been to so many interviews that I'd lost track of which one she actually wanted.

'I'm going to be working at your school, helping those kids that find school a bit hard. I have to start next week because I have to do a special training week and a first-aid course too,' she said excitedly.

'At MY school?'

'Well, yes, but on the other side of the building, Zack. You won't know I'm there, I promise.'

I turned round and slammed my bedroom door. As if it wasn't hard enough. Now my mum, who wears the most ridiculous clothes and has hair that she dyes crazy colours, was going to be right there at my new school. Just when things seemed like they might just be a little less bad, a little less than totally awful, she goes and ruins it.

'Zack.'

'Just leave me alone, would you?' I shouted at the door and then I kind of punched it so hard that for a minute I really thought I'd broken my thumb or something, and I had to bite my lip to stop myself from crying out.

'Zack, please?'

I picked up the photograph frame of me, Mum and Dad. I felt so angry I thought I was going to smash it against the wall. I let it drop to the floor and, with my best left-footed cross, I booted it under the bed.

'Zack, please don't be mad. It'll be OK.'

I didn't answer, but, when I looked out of the window at the blue sky and sea that was pancake flat, I knew exactly what I was going to do.

15

Alice

I fell asleep holding the photograph, but when I woke up it was on my bedside table propped up against my books. I climbed out of bed and I pulled back the curtains. The sky was so blue it looked like someone had just painted it, and the sea was so flat it looked like glass. The beach. I just had to go again. I never normally did things I wasn't supposed to, but I couldn't help it. I felt as though something was almost tugging at me to go back. Besides, it wasn't as though they needed me. I was just deciding what to take when I suddenly realised I would have to come up with a way to explain what I was doing. I was just thinking about how I was going to get away when I heard shouting from the hallway.

'David! David! Hurry! HURRY! Your daughter doesn't want to wait until the end of August!'

I opened the door and saw Mum bent over with her hands pressed to the wall. Then she screamed. It was so loud and so scary I thought she'd broken a bone or something worse.

Dad came running up the stairs, but he had a huge smile on his face, and when he saw me looking scared he laughed and said, 'Don't worry, Alice. This is all perfectly normal. Your sister clearly wants to be born now!'

So that is what happened. My little sister arrived into this world on August 5th, but I was nowhere to be found. I had packed a bag and run away.

The walk down to the beach wasn't as scary as the first time. I didn't nearly slip and I carefully jumped over the ledge, holding tightly on to my bag. Actually, I almost marched all the way. It was a grumpy, angry sort of a stomp, and all the time I was thinking about how Mum and Dad didn't need me now they had their baby. My sister was going to have my cot. Mum wanted me to give her my cuddly toys and she was going to get my clothes too.

When we were packing for Scotland, I saw Mum fold away some of the clothes that were too small for me because one day my sister would be able to have them. Later that night, I'd crept down the hallway where I'd found the big box of clothes and I pulled out my favourite blue jumper. She was NOT having that as well.

When I got down to the beach, I took my shoes off so that I could feel the warm sand between my toes. I tucked the shoes inside my bag and, with a long stick, I swiped through the air to make a loud zipping noise. It was already pretty hot and I was pleased that I'd remembered to pack a little umbrella to give some shade. I found the big rock where I'd seen the strange boy sitting, and I set my bag down and laid out the towel. It was the perfect kind of day to be on the beach and I decided that I would lie in the sun until I was so hot I couldn't bear it any more. Until I was so stinking hot I'd have to run down the sand and jump into the cool blue waters and swim in the shallow turquoise lagoon.

But I was not alone.

I heard him before I saw him. He was singing. I think I knew the song, but I couldn't be sure. This time the tide was in so he must have swum round the headland and then climbed on to the big rock. I thought no one could do that. I didn't know it was possible. I looked again as he slid down from the last rock and waded knee-deep through the shallow waters of the lagoon and, when he looked up in my direction, I quickly darted behind the rock so he couldn't see me. But I found myself peeping out and watching him like I did last time. What was he doing here?

He slowly walked along the shoreline, occasionally bending down to look at shells, and that was the moment I realised that it was the boy who had moved into the coastguard cottage. It was the boy who had been shouting at his mum. The one Dad had said looked like trouble. I suddenly felt a bit scared and hid further behind the rock. What if he was going to be horrible to me?

I peeped back out from the rock to check, but he was gone.

For a second or two I didn't move and then I spied the stick I'd found at the top of the beach and quickly grabbed it. I stood up slowly and quietly, gripping the stick tightly in my hand, and when I came out from my hiding place I saw him sitting at the water's edge. This was supposed to be our private beach. I wanted to be here alone. He had no right to trespass. With that angry thought in my head, I walked down the beach with my weapon in the air, but as I got closer I could hear he was humming a tune I knew. As I got closer, my stride slowed down until I was almost creeping up on him. When I was about an arm's length away, I stopped, he turned round and I saw his face once again. It was just like I remembered, but it was more bronzed and his nose was a little red from sunburn. He looked up and smiled. I lowered my arm and the stick that I'd been waving in the air like a crazy person. I stood there for some time, just looking at him. I watched him pick up a pretty pink shell and turn it over in his hand.

'Wow, you kind of look like Pocahontas,' he said to me.

I said nothing. I had expected him to shout or be mean or something.

'Are you from Culver Manor?'

I nodded.

'So this is your very own private beach?'

I nodded again.

'Are you here on your own?'

I nodded.

His voice was different from those of the boys I knew at school. It sounded a bit deeper or something.

'I'm sorry; I know I'm not supposed to be here. It's just . . . Well . . . Mum told me there would be beaches here – ha, another thing she lied about.' I heard an angry sound to his voice, but then he stopped talking and looked back down at his hands.

I waited for what seemed like forever and then he turned back to me, smiled and said very slowly and clearly, 'I am Zack.'

Without really thinking, I picked up the stick and, using it like a pencil, I drew in the sand: *I am Alice*.

16

Zack

'Open the door, Zack.' She turned the handle, but I'd already locked it. 'Zack, please.' I ignored her. 'You know this is really hard for me too. This is really hard for us both.' I heard her crying again and this time I didn't feel sorry for her. I felt angry with her.

'What are you talking about? Hard for you? How is it just as hard for you? You don't have to start a new school where everyone will already have friends like I used to,' I shouted. 'How is it hard for you?'

'Zack, please,' I heard her snivel, but that's the moment when I did the swearing thing again. I could have said get lost or something, but the word just came out again and I held my breath. She said nothing. There was a long silence where I think I could just about hear her breathing on the other side of the door.

Then she sort of whispered something I'd never heard her say. 'My father always used to say you can learn a great deal about a boy from the way he treats his mother.' I heard her footsteps on the stairs and the front door as it closed behind her. I sat down on my bed and sighed, but when I heard a seagull outside I remembered the beach and the flying rucksack.

This time I packed a bag and I felt excited as I headed off out of the village, beyond the harbour and along the stony beach, but, as I got to the giant boulder, I realised that this time the tide was so far in that the only way to reach Culver Cove was to swim there and that meant leaving my bag and the food I'd brought with me. I stood there for a while, watching the water. I remembered what my mum had told me about the dangerous undercurrent and I shivered a little bit when I imagined myself being dragged out to sea. I could have waited, but I didn't. I should have been sensible, but I wasn't, and instead I hid my bag behind some rocks and set off.

I could say the water was really cold, but it wasn't: it was totally freezing and my skin quickly became numb. I swam quickly and when I reached a large rock that was sticking out of the water I climbed on top of it to rest a while. That's when I saw the first seal. I watched it dive under the water, popping back up to the surface a minute or two later. *Wow*, I thought. It flipped over on to its back and was so close I could almost touch its whiskers and, when I looked down at its big round eyes, it reminded me of Otter so much it made me smile.

It made me think of the time Dad and I had been sailing together and a load of dolphins had swum right alongside the boat. 'It's like they're watching out for us, Zack,' he'd said to me. 'It's as though they're steering us in the right direction.'

I watched the seal swim further and further out, but then it stopped and seemed to watch me. I felt like it was telling me to be careful; it felt as though Dad was right: it was watching out for me so, while it could still see me, I slid back into the water and swam as fast as I could and I didn't stop until I rounded the headland.

I pulled myself on to the last rock, lay flat on my back and waited until I'd got my breath back. I had made it. When the time came to go home, the tide would probably be out. I could just walk back then, it would be easy, and, as I looked back towards the perfect sandy cove, I prayed that this time I'd be alone.

I was so wrong.

I walked along the beach, but I couldn't see anyone. I even looked up to make sure there weren't any more flying Barbie bags and eventually I sat down at the edge of the water with my back to the waterfall. The skin on the tip of my nose was burnt, my stomach was telling me I needed to eat and then my dad's favourite song popped into my head. The words always made Mum laugh because my dad was the happiest, smiliest person you ever met. I never saw him sad and I never, ever saw him cry. I thought of the words again: 'I'd like to be unhappy, but I really don't have the time.' I was just humming the tune when I sensed someone behind me. My skin prickled and my heart beat quickly, but when I turned round I saw it was her again. The girl from last time.

Her black hair was longer than I remembered, she seemed a bit older too, and when I smiled up at her she lowered the stick she'd been waving in the air. She reminded me of a mini Pocahontas and when I blurted that out I felt really stupid, but she didn't say anything; she just stared like she did the last time.

I expected her to tell me to leave, but she didn't. She didn't say a word and when I asked her if she was here by herself she just nodded. In fact, every time I asked her a question, she just nodded.

The odd thing was, when I looked up into her big brown eyes, it was as though I knew her and that had never happened to me before. I muttered something about my mum and when she still didn't say a word I wondered if she was from another country or something. I can speak a bit of French and a tiny bit of Spanish. Whenever we went on holiday, my dad would do this really embarrassing thing of talking English loudly, slowly, but with a sort of accent that made him sound completely silly. It used to make Mum and I laugh because he didn't even realise he was doing it.

I looked up at the girl again. *Perhaps she doesn't even speak*

English, I thought, so I turned back to her, smiled and said very slowly: 'I am Zack.'

She took the stick she was holding and wrote in the sand, *I am Alice*.

17

Alice

Me and Zack stayed on the beach until the sun got cooler and the tide had gone out. I don't know how long we were there together, but we'd already swum out to the rocks twice, eaten my picnic and played noughts and crosses in the sand when Zack suddenly sat up.

'Best get home,' he said, pulling on his grey hoody.

I nodded. I knew I'd be in big trouble if Mum and Dad found out I'd come to Culver Cove again and I wanted to be able to sneak back into the garden without being noticed, and then I realised something which made me feel strange. Mum and Dad always let me just go off in the garden for hours. They know I can spend all day making up a magical world in the walled garden, they know I can spend hours trying to make perfume out of the rose petals, but they always

105

asked me loads of questions when I got home. They always wanted to know what I'd been doing and what adventures I'd had, but recently they hadn't been doing that. Now they didn't ask me anything and I knew why. They didn't care. They didn't care about me any more.

'Alice,' said Zack and I looked up at him. 'Alice, will you tell? I mean, like, will I get into trouble?'

Would I tell? No way, I thought, *I'm not Casper. I'm not a telltale at all.* I frowned at him and tried to get the words out. I wanted to say, 'Cross my heart and hope to die,' but in the end I just raised my finger to my lips and drew a cross over my chest.

'Awesome!' he said and I watched him clamber over the rocks, and before he jumped down off the last enormous boulder he turned round and waved.

Zack Drake, I thought as I climbed back up the path towards the waterfall. Zack Ethan Drake who told me that he used to have a dog called Otter and I wanted to ask what happened to it. I've always wanted a dog, but Dad won't let me. He actually got quite cross the last time. He suddenly sighed, stood up from the kitchen table and said, 'No means no.' The really weird thing is that Florence said that Aunt Aggy had said the exact same thing to her about getting a dog, but, when she had asked her mum to tell her why, Aunt Aggy said something about an accident, but she wouldn't tell Florence any more. It was really weird.

As I wandered back along the path, I started to feel scared. What if Mum and Dad knew where I was? What if I got caught? Then another thought came into my head. A much worse thought. I had forgotten all about it. Being on the beach with Zack had been so much fun that I hadn't thought about the horrid thing that was happening. *Urgh*, I thought. My soon-to-be little sister was sure to be there by now. I felt my heart sink and my legs get slower and slower until I was standing in front of the gate, but I couldn't move any further. Culver Manor would not be *my* special place any more. I was going to have to share it and I didn't like the way that made me feel. It made me angry and sad and I knew, right then and there, that everything was about to be very different.

No sooner had I closed the door behind me than I heard shouting. I heard my dad calling my name and I knew I had to run really fast before he saw me. I raced back through the orchard, the rose garden, the walled garden, along the side of the tennis court and, by the time I reached the cedar tree, I was panting and gasping for breath.

'Alice! Alice!'

Dad was standing on the terrace at the back of the house and I just had time to change direction so that it looked as though I was walking up the lawn instead.

'Alice – there you are! I've been looking all over for you! Come on, your sister has arrived!'

I looked up at my smiling dad and, as I walked up the hill towards the terrace, I saw that he was grinning his big Christmas Day grin. I thought about how Mum and Dad always used to say that the day I arrived was the happiest day of their lives and I got slower and slower. Was this going to be the happiest day of their lives instead? It felt as though the ground was sinking beneath my feet and when I looked back up towards him I thought I was going to cry.

'Come on, Alice, don't drag your heels. This is a happy, happy day.'

I followed him back inside through the hallway and up the stairs to my parents' bedroom. It's a big bedroom and has the sort of princess bed you sometimes see in fairy-tale books. Mum says it's called a four–poster, but Dad calls it her Sleeping Beauty bed and it's so big and tall that I have to climb on to a little stool to reach it. It has these heavy red and yellow curtains that you can pull all the way round it, and when me and Florence were little Mum let us sleep in it sometimes when she stayed with us.

I walked across the wooden floor until my toes touched the rug at the foot of the bed and I peered over the mountain of white towels, sheets and blankets. Mum looked hot and sweaty, and her cheeks were so pink I thought she might be ill. She sat up slowly, holding a finger to her lips, but I didn't see a little sister at all. I just saw a white bundle of blankets and then Mum held out her hand towards me. For a while I didn't move at all. I didn't want to look. If I didn't look, I could pretend it wasn't there, just like my dad once told me to do when I got really upset about a spider in the corner of the bathroom.

'Pretend he's not there,' he'd whispered when I pointed at the large eight-legged creature that was hiding on the other side of the toilet. 'Pretend he's not there and you don't need to be scared.' It had worked, sort of. And, as I had my hair washed and splashed around in the bath, I did forget all about the spider.

As I stood next to Mum's bed, I tried to do the same thing. I kept my head up and tried not to look down at the white bundle that was moving. Then it made a noise, a gurgling kind of cry, and Mum held the thing up higher so that it was lying on her chest and I could see its face.

I must have been frowning really hard because Mum said, 'Alice, come here, don't frown. She's beautiful, isn't she?'

I peered over the covers to take a better look and stared at my sister for the very first time. Her eyes were closed tightly and her tiny hands rested on my mum's finger so that I could see just how little she was. She was so small. Smaller than I thought she'd be.

Had I been that small? Had I lain on my other mother like she did? I knew I was born on a rainy day. I had been taken away immediately from my other mother, but my little sister was born into a bath of golden sunlight and was able to sleep next to her REAL mother in a beautiful princess bed. It made my hands clench into fists, and a feeling that I had never felt before got bigger and bigger in my stomach, so big that I knew all I wanted to do was turn round, run out and never look at her again.

I stayed in my bedroom until the sun went down and the sky was so dark and clear that the moon lit up the garden below. Dad begged me to come and have some dinner with him, but I didn't want to. I just shook my head and in the end he left a tray of sandwiches outside my room. I heard him talking on the telephone and realised quickly that it must be Aunt Aggy so I went to the door and listened.

'But Alice won't talk at all. There's nothing wrong with her and we've tried everything. Sophie said that, when she went in to see the baby, she wouldn't go anywhere near her or the baby. She said she just glared at her so much that it scared her a bit. It's just jealousy. Alice is jealous . . .'

I didn't hear anything else because I ran back to my bed, grabbed the photograph from the table and jumped under the duvet. I didn't hear Dad softly knock at my door. I didn't hear the words he said or feel him stroke my back as I cried.

Was I jealous? Was that what this horrid feeling was?

Mum and Dad like to talk about feelings a lot. They say that it's better to show a little of what you're feeling than bottle it all up inside. Mum once told me that if you were feeling sad and you wanted to cry you should just cry until the feeling stopped. Dad said he would much rather I shout and stomp around a bit when I'm cross than sulk in silence, and when I asked why they said: 'If you don't cry when you need to or get angry when you have to, you won't ever know how.'

But I hadn't spoken for six months so I hadn't told them how I was feeling. I didn't even know *what* the feeling was until now, and Mum once told me that being jealous was not a good thing to be. AT ALL. She said it was a very bad thing to be. I once heard her say to Dad that jealous people can be the worst kind of people, and I remember it really well because I was eating an apple at the time.

'When someone starts feeling jealous,' she'd said, 'they find it hard to stop. It sort of eats them up like a worm inside an apple.'

Was I the worm inside the apple? Or was the jealous thing like a worm inside me? Would Mum and Dad want to send me back to the place where they'd chosen me from?

I suddenly felt very afraid. Remembering what Mum had told me about Dad and Aunt Aggy. I felt a fizzing noise in my head. Would they send me back?

18

Alice

That night I cried myself to sleep, but then my little sister cried me awake and she did that every night for five nights. Mum and Dad looked so tired that they stumbled around the kitchen as though they were still asleep. The only good thing about them being so distracted was I got to sneak out of the house and run down to Culver Cove nearly every day, where I could forget all about the screaming, crying little sister who so far didn't have a name.

Mum and Dad said they couldn't decide. They said I was an Alice from the moment they saw me, but they just couldn't agree what my little sister should be called which was fine by me. They had the screaming baby and I had the beach.

Zack always turned up after me, and even though at first I was angry to see him there, the more we met, the more I realised that him being there with me made the cove even better. He's told me nearly everything about himself. Actually, he talks quite a lot, for a boy that is. He told me that he was named after a world-famous mountain climber and when he told me that it was a bit like he kind of wanted me to be impressed or something.

But there are so many times when I want to ask questions. Like the time he told me about kicking a policeman. I wanted to say something to make him feel better. I wanted to say that I'd never been on a plane, but might be scared to. I wanted to ask if he'd said sorry or what happened when they missed the plane. I wanted to, but the best I could do was to look like I didn't understand. Only that didn't work and I had to listen to him tell me the whole story all over again and it sounded even crazier the second time around. So I got out the notebook and after I drew a really rubbish picture of a shell I wrote another list.

Things I like about Zack
He doesn't ask me why I'm not talking.
He doesn't make fun of me when I won't jump off the
   rocks.
He's an amazing swimmer.
He found the perfect pink shell on the beach AND he let
   me have it.
He has really nice eyes.
He tells funny stories about things and places I've never
   heard of.

113

Things I don't like about Zack

He talks a bit too much.

He farts and burps too much.

He sometimes says mean things about his mum.

He doesn't like watermelon.

He is VERY greedy.

One day, towards the end of our first week on the beach, I watched him climb on to the large rock.

'Alice, come here quickly!' he shouted at me.

I put my drawing book down and ran across to him. He helped me up on to the rock and I realised that while he was quite small for a boy that was nearly thirteen he was very strong. He helped me on to the top of the boulder where we both sat side by side with the sun on our faces.

'Look! Look, Alice, the seals that led me here are back,' he whispered, pointing at a black shape in the water.

I squinted and after a moment two roundish grey and black heads popped up from the water and started swimming on their backs towards us.

'Come on then!' And with that Zack slid into the water towards the seals, but I didn't. I can swim really well, I've got all my badges and everything, but as the seals got closer I could see that they were a lot bigger than they'd seemed. I wasn't so sure I wanted to be too close. I watched them dive under the water alongside Zack. It's like he's a mermaid boy or something. I don't know anyone that can hold their breath as long as he can, or do backflips off the rocks, or cartwheel off them into the sea like he does.

Whenever we would meet, Zack didn't say much about me not speaking, but he sometimes said he wished his mum wouldn't talk so much. Actually, he said quite a few mean things about his mum and the cottage that they were living in. Sometimes I wondered if he wanted to just run all the way back to London and his best friend Lou.

A week after my sister with no name was born, I got down to Culver Cove a bit later than normal. Zack was already there and he had brought something with him. I put my rucksack down and walked over to where he was standing.

'This is a bodyboard, Alice. We're gonna have a blast.'

I grinned back at him and that afternoon we spent the whole time surfing into the shore, being dunked under waves and getting salty seawater up our noses, but I didn't care. I didn't care that the sand was in my ears or that I had sunburn on the tops of my ears. And I was really proud when Zack watched me spin round on the body-board all the way to the shore and he sort of jumped up in the air.

'Whoop! Whoop! Alice, you're a proper surfer now!'

Zack is very greedy. Even when he brings twice the amount of food as I do, he nearly always wants some of my picnic too, but one day he didn't bring anything to eat. I wandered down the beach to look for shells and when I got back Zack had gobbled nearly my entire picnic and in his hand he had my notebook. I watched him stuff the last Jaffa cake into his mouth and then he burst out laughing.

'Ha!' he said, looking up. 'I have nice eyes, do I?' He fluttered his eyelashes.

I felt my cheeks get hot, but Zack just laughed and laughed.

'Ooh, Alice thinks I have nice eyes!' he said in a silly voice, dancing round the towel. Before I knew what I was doing, I had grabbed the notebook out of his greedy hands and smacked him over the head with it.

'Oh my God, Alice, that really hurt! Are you mental?'

I said nothing and started packing my stuff away.

'For God's sake, Alice! I was only teasing!'

I turned round and glared at him, but I felt my bottom lip trembling.

'Typical!' he shouted. 'Typical girl! Can't take a little joke! How am I supposed to know what you're like if you don't even speak, you total lunatic!'

A lunatic? What was a lunatic? Was that someone that was crazy? I felt myself get more upset. I tried to blink away the tears, but it was too late.

'Oh great! Great!' Zack sort of sighed, looked up at the sky and raised his hands in a way that made him look like he was totally fed up. 'Go on! Cry! Cry if you like. I'm used to it. Mum's always crying. But you won't see me cry!' he said, getting angrier and more shouty with each word. 'My dad never cried and I'm not about to start either! I'm not as brave as him, I never will be, but he always used to say that sometimes being really brave is saying the thing that you're too scared to say. So here's the real truth, Alice! You need to grow up and stop being such a baby. I don't know why you've decided not to speak, but it's pretty damn stupid. It's stupid and childish and I can't be bothered with it!'

We stood on the beach, staring at each other for ages. The tears rolled down my cheeks and I saw Zack's angry face frowning deeper and his hands clenched so tightly into fists that the skin went sort of white.

I almost said something. I opened my mouth to speak and this time I realised that I could. I just didn't know which words to use first. I wiped the tears from my face and looked up at him once more, but a dark shadow came across his face and I felt scared, so I picked up my bag and went and sat on the other side of the beach next to the waterfall. Every so often I looked over at him, but when he tried to say something I put my hands over my ears. We sat like that for ages, but when the tide started coming back in Zack got up and left without saying goodbye.

But I didn't want to go home and back to the crying baby so I sat on the beach, watching the tide come in.

Finally I realised I had to go home, or they'd discover I was missing and ask lots of questions, so I stomped up the path quickly, swatting flies away from my sticky, sweaty face. When I got to the little stone seat, I was so hot and out of breath I had to sit down and rest for a while. I could just make out the top of Zack's head as he scrambled along the stony beach back towards the harbour, and I felt a bit bad that we'd left each other in such a bad mood.

I dusted the sand off my legs, shoes and bag, so that there'd be no beachy evidence, and then I reached out to open the garden door. I tried to turn it, but it wouldn't budge. I tried again and still it wouldn't move. I pulled and twisted, but it was stuck. The rusty old bolt was stuck! My heart started pounding and I felt sort of sick. How could I get back into the house? How would I sneak back in without being caught? I looked at the walls on either side of the door; I'd never be able to climb up there. They were twice as high as the boulder on the beach and I'd needed Zack to help me get on top of that.

I felt panicked and scared and I tried to shout for help, but it was as though a giant was pressing down on my throat. If Mum and Dad knew I'd been to the beach, I'd be in trouble. So much trouble they'd stop me leaving the house at all, and then I'd never see the cove again. What was I going to do? I looked for a way round the door, then I heard the waves crashing on to the beach below and suddenly I had an idea. I could walk round the headland just like Zack! So I turned and quickly ran back down the path towards the cove where I could follow Zack's footsteps back to the harbour, through the village and be home in no time.

As soon as I got down to the shore, I saw there was a big problem. As I ran down the beach towards the water, my heart sank. The tide was now really high and I could only just see the top of the boulder that Zack had climbed over. What was I going to do? I was locked out of the garden and now I was trapped on the beach! I took my rucksack off and sat down at the edge of the water. Perhaps I could wait until the tide went back out and I could walk safely round the rocks. Perhaps someone would unlock the door and I could sneak in through the garden again. I sat for ages trying to decide what to do and then I suddenly spied a black shape by the headland. I stood up to get a better look. It was a seal. One of them had come back. Zack had said that they'd guided him here, so perhaps it was telling me what to do too?

I looked back up the beach to the waterfall and decided that if I wanted to get home I was going to have to be brave. I would have to swim faster than I'd ever swum before. So, carefully, I tucked my rucksack behind one of the rocks at the top of the beach and, with one eye on the seal, I waded into the water and set off for the headland.

I tried breaststroke because that's my favourite, but the water kept splashing into my eyes and in the end I ducked my head under the water like Zack always did. I kicked and splashed as fast as I could. I had my thousand-metre swimming badge, I could swim a long way, but this was different. It felt like I wasn't really getting anywhere. I took a big gulp of air and saw the tip of the boulder. *Not much further*, I thought, *just a little more*. I saw the seal out of the corner of my eye, but it dived under the water and disappeared. It was leaving me! I was alone in the dark, deep and cold waters.

My heart beat even faster and my legs felt as if they were being pulled down and down. It was like my arms couldn't move, no matter how hard I tried. A hot, searing pain shot up and down my legs until I couldn't kick any more. My body started to sink under the water. Panicking, I took one last gulp of air before my head went under. I saw the surface get further away and then everything went silent.

19

Zack

After those first few times on the beach, me and Alice became sort of friends, well, as much of a friend as you can be with someone that doesn't actually talk. I don't really mind. I've never been 'almost friends' with a girl before. The thing is, because she doesn't talk, I find that I chat a lot. Like Mum does; it's really weird. I think I've told Alice nearly everything about me, but she never looks like she's bored or anything. And sometimes I notice she looks at me when I've said something as though she's confused.

One day we were sitting on the beach with our toes in the water when I noticed a bruise on her leg and it made me think about how I'd kicked the policeman at the airport. And for some reason the whole story just came blurting out of me, but when I looked at Alice she wasn't shocked or anything. She just looked like she hadn't understood a word of what I'd said, so I repeated the whole story again and, when I did that, I felt weird. As I heard myself tell the story once more, I felt totally stupid. Why hadn't I just told Mum why I didn't want to go in an aeroplane ever again? Why had I waited till I got to the airport before having some total 'kicking a policeman' meltdown?

Alice tells me some things by writing in this notebook that she carries everywhere. Usually she hides it, but one day I had a look when she was having a swim. She's really good at drawing actually. And her handwriting is way nicer than mine, but I think all girls' handwriting is better than boys'. It's like they're just made to fiddle around with pens and biros like I'd seen Lexi and her friend Eddie doing for hours.

When I reached over to put the notebook back, a photograph fell out of the pages. I checked to see if Alice was looking and when I saw her duck under the water I took a closer look. I could see straight away that it had to be Alice's mum. They were so alike. The exact same eyes and hair. I didn't have a chance to look any more because I heard Alice splashing in the water as if she was getting out so I quickly put the photo and notebook away.

When I was walking back from the beach that day, I thought that if all the girls at Somerset Vale were like Alice it might not be so bad. I was just wondering how many girls there would be in my new class when I heard a familiar noise. A chugging sound that I knew so well. The noise got louder and louder and I turned to look up at the sky. At first the last of the sunlight was shining too brightly into my eyes to see it properly, but as it came closer and closer I saw it. A plane. A little blue plane. I thought of Dad once again and a smile came across my face as I followed it with my eyes.

When I got home, I was feeling strange. Not happy, not really sad, but as though someone had just given me a brand-new guitar and then told me I wasn't allowed to play it. Mum was sitting in the living room, watching some rubbish soap.

'Are you OK, sweetheart?'

I said nothing. I wasn't in the mood for talking and besides it felt like I'd done nothing but talk all day. But Mum wouldn't leave me alone. Where had I been? What had I been doing all afternoon? Had I eaten? Could I pick my clothes off my bedroom floor? When did I have a shower last? What did I want for dinner? Would I like a new bag for school? On and on she went. Question after question. It made me think of Alice and the fact that she could go for days without talking at all.

'What would make someone not be able to talk?' I said suddenly.

Mum eyed me suspiciously. 'What makes you ask that?'

I shrugged my shoulders. 'No reason,' I said, trying to look like it was just an ordinary, everyday, Zack-type question, but my mum kept looking at me really strangely.

'Is it because you've met Alice? The girl that lives up at Culver Manor. Apparently, she just stopped talking.'

'No. I've not met anyone,' I snapped. 'I just wondered, that's all.'

She looked right at me as if to say, 'I so know when you're lying.' Then she walked out of the room and I could hear her rummaging through the cupboard under the stairs. She came back into the room with a large shoebox.

'Here,' she said, holding out a photograph she'd shown me before of her, Granddad and the other kids outside the cottage. I looked at the two older-looking boys and the girl, but then I spotted another face peeping out from behind my granddad that I hadn't seen last time. There he was, a smaller skinny-looking boy with dimples and a mass of curly hair which seemed to spring up in every direction.

'Yeah,' I said, 'you showed me this already.'

'Well, that's David, Dr Richardson,' she said, pointing at one of the older boys. 'He's Alice's dad. We used to be friends.'

I looked at the photograph more closely. Alice's dad was grinning and underneath his arm he held a football. Alice definitely didn't look like her dad, but the other taller boy and the girl in the photograph looked just like him.

'Who's that then?' I asked, pointing at the taller of the two boys.

Mum looked sad when she answered. 'That's Tom. David's older brother. They were always hanging out down at the harbour when we were young. And that,' she said, pointing at the other girl, 'is Aggy, David's little sister.'

'And him?' I asked, pointing at the curly-haired boy.

Mum suddenly looked really sad. She held the photograph up to the light and sighed. 'He was my favourite. The sweetest, kindest boy I ever knew.' She sort of gazed off into a bit of a daydream and I thought that she was going to cry. I waited for her to tell me more, but she started searching through the box until she pulled out a much larger photograph that I hadn't seen before.

'Culver Manor,' she said, holding it out to me, and I saw a house that looked almost as big as my old school. The front of it was covered in some kind of plant thing that made the house look green. The windows were boarded up and the whole place made me think that it was somewhere I wouldn't want to live in at all. *Poor Alice*, I thought, *she lives in a well creepy house.*

'I don't know what it looks like these days, but the last time I went there it looked like this.' Mum stopped to think for a bit and then she shook her head slowly and said, 'That house was filled with sadness; that family had such bad luck.'

'What bad luck?' Suddenly I was really interested in the spooky house that Alice lived in. 'Tell me! What happened?' But Mum put the photograph back in the box and stood up.

'Oh, another time, Zack. I'm not in the mood for telling sad tales after all. What do you want for your dinner?'

I watched her disappear into the kitchen and for a minute I was going to ask again, but then one of those stupid 'Back to school' adverts came on and I thought about the new school again. A feeling of dread started to crawl over me. I imagined the classroom filled with kids that all knew each other. I saw myself walking into the canteen and dropping my plate. I imagined everyone laughing at me and when Mum brought us a bowl of pasta each I didn't feel much like eating mine.

'Zack, if you do happen to meet Alice, you will be nice, won't you?'

I ignored her and carried on pushing a piece of pasta round the bowl. I could feel her looking at me and when she saw my miserable face and the half-eaten pasta she said that if I wanted to I could run over to the shop and get some chocolate.

'Don't run through the churchyard!' she shouted after me as I raced over the little bridge.

That night, when I was just about to turn my light out, Mum knocked at the door and peered inside. I looked at the floor that was covered in clothes, a plate from three days ago, a heap of wet towels and several empty crisp packets.

'Come on, Zack. I asked you to clear this mess up two days ago.' She walked in, almost tripped over a pair of shoes and sighed. 'Look, you're going to have to be a bit more grown-up about stuff like this. How would you like it if I left the house in a tip?'

Why couldn't she just leave me alone?

'I couldn't care less, Mum, I really couldn't.' And with that I turned and lay back on the bed and opened a magazine to tell her the conversation was now over.

She stood over me for ages, tapping her foot like eleventy million times.

'Your dad would be so sad to hear you talk to me like this.'

'Well, he isn't here, is he?' I said angrily. 'And now we're stuck here, aren't we?'

She didn't say anything after that so I just carried on looking at my magazine, hoping she'd leave me alone.

'Zack,' she said seriously, 'I know this is really difficult. If I was you, I'd be cross with me too. But listen, if you carry on with that attitude, you're going to be really unhappy. If you talk to other people like that, you're going to get in trouble. If you kick off every time I ask you to help me, we're both going to be miserable and, more importantly, if you go to your new school with this rubbish "poor old me" attitude, you won't have any friends.'

I put down my magazine and glared at her. 'Have you finished?'

She looked down at me with a sort of surprised, shocked face.

'OK, fine, be like that, but do me a favour, will you? Try and stay out of trouble when I go to work on Tuesday. Please? Just . . . I don't know, be cool, would you?'

Like Mum knew what that meant.

Mum and her ever-changing hair colour which was like: THE OPPOSITE OF COOL.

20

Zack

Yesterday Mum went to work and I got to stay in the house all by myself. Well, almost all by myself because Mum had arranged for this woman she's known for years to keep checking up on me. She said that she wasn't sure it was such a good idea to let me hang around all day by myself. 'Who *knows* what you'll get up to?' she'd said when I asked her why.

'This is Pippa,' she said to me on Tuesday morning. Pippa wore the sort of clothes that a man would wear: a pair of dark blue shorts with lots of pockets, a sort of big black belt that had a purse at the front and a pair of heavy-looking sandals that showed all her toes were kind of muddled up and sticking out. I didn't like the look of her at all so I stared at her with my 'I don't like you already' face. And she peered

128

over her glasses at me in a 'you look like trouble' kind of way. She chatted to Mum for a while so I went upstairs to clean my teeth. I was just thinking about when I could sneak out and down to the beach when Mum came barging into the bathroom.

'Leapfrogging over gravestones is NOT ON at all, Zack!'

Oh, I thought, remembering the short cut I'd taken through the churchyard the other night. *Oops.* Then she went off on one about how it was a really disrespectful thing to do and that Granddad was buried there and how unkindly I was behaving. She said how lucky we were to live here and how I needed to make an effort.

'"Centre of the universe," my dad used to say! And you know what, Zack? Being here again makes me realise that this is a much better place for you to grow up. It's safer. People look out for each other. People care about each other.' I heard a tremble in her voice and I felt bad.

When Mum left for work, Pippa sort of hung around for a bit, asking lots of stupid questions. I looked up at her from the sofa and sort of grunted back at her.

'Hmm,' she said, peering over her glasses. 'My grandson is about your age. He's football mad. I bet you're like that too?'

I thought of Lou and the hours of football we'd played together in our old garden. It made me think of Dad and his ability to save just about any goal we tried. I'm not very good really.

'My dad played for his school and stuff, but I'm not . . .' I drifted off, but Pippa just smiled down at me kindly.

'Well, my husband says I'm a pretty bad cook, but I've not poisoned anyone yet. I left a casserole in the oven last year and forgot all about it. Came back from the beach and the thing was a lump of black bones in the bottom of the pan. Stunk the whole house out for weeks. Even the dog seemed to turn his nose up, as if to say, "Good gracious, Pippa, when are you going to learn to cook properly?"'

It made me laugh, sort of, then she ruffled the top of my hair and left, saying she'd be back at lunchtime. I watched her waddle across the little bridge and that's when I realised that I quite liked being left in the house by myself. At our old house, in our old life, my mum had to come everywhere with me and I was never, ever allowed to just stay home alone. Back then I didn't mind, I didn't really like sitting on my own, but now I loved having the little cottage all to myself where I could stay in my pyjamas, watch TV and eat cereal out of the box without anyone telling me what to do.

The next morning I ate three bowls of cereal, two slices of toast and by the time Pippa came over to check on me I'd already eaten my lunch and the last bag of crisps so there was nothing left to take to the beach at all. I watched her cross the bridge again and as soon as she was out of sight I headed out once more.

The thing about Alice is she brings the best picnics to the beach. She always has much nicer sandwiches and cakes and biscuits than me, and most of the time she lets me have some of hers too. We must have been there for about an hour or so when I watched Alice wander off down the beach and at that exact moment I felt my tummy rumble. I was so hungry that it actually hurt a bit. Do you ever get that? Anyway, I know I shouldn't have done it, but the lovely foodie smells that were coming out of Barbie world were too nice to ignore and, before I knew what I was doing, I'd stuffed nearly all of Alice's Jaffa cakes in my greedy mouth. I was just finishing the last one when I spied her notebook. It was opened at a page, and I saw she'd written my name, so I bent down and picked up the book. At the top of the page she'd written: **Things I like about Zack**, and then there was a sort of list. It kind of made me smile a bit. But, when I got to the bit where she'd written *He has really nice eyes*, it made me laugh out loud and boy, was she unhappy about it.

At first I thought she was going to kick sand in my face or something. I thought she'd really shout at me; instead she grabbed the notebook out of my hand and smacked me over the head with it. I'm not kidding. And it wasn't some little girly smack either: it was a proper whack and it totally hurt. I thought she was completely mental. I mean, I was only teasing, but she, like, lost the plot. Then she started crying and it made me get angry. You don't catch me crying every five minutes and I just blurted out a load of stuff to her that I knew I shouldn't have.

She did that typical girly, pouty, sulky thing and went off in a huff. She sat at the other end of the beach for ages and after a while I felt really bad. I called out to say I was sorry, but she just put her hands over her ears like some kind of baby. I was going to go over to her and say sorry again, I really was, but I realised that the tide was starting to come in and I'd have to leave before it got too dangerous.

I really didn't ever want to do that scary swim again.

I wandered back slowly. I felt the sunburn on my nose and started to pick the skin off from around the edges. I had just reached the other side of the headland when I heard the chugging sound again. It got louder and louder, and when I looked up towards the other side of the bay I could just see the little blue plane soaring high above the hill. It flew higher and higher, and I watched it get further and further out to sea until it became a smudge and disappeared. I stood like that for a while, kind of hoping it would come back, but it didn't.

My legs felt tired so I sat down on one of the larger flat stones, stared out to sea and thought about Dad. How do you get to be brave like he was? Is it something I'd learn like cricket or tennis? Is it something that would just happen? Like the time my school shoes were too small and Mum had said, 'My goodness, Zack, your feet must have grown overnight.'

I looked back towards the headland. I watched the waves as they crashed on to the stony beach, but then I saw something else. At first I thought it was just seagulls diving into the sea, then I thought it was the seal again, and finally I realised it was none of those things. The shape that was splashing around in the water was Alice. What was she doing? Why was she swimming so far out? Then I saw with horror that she WAS NOT SWIMMING. Alice was drowning! I saw her head dip under the water and pop up again. She waved her arms around in the air and all the time she was getting further and further away. She was being dragged out to sea! If I didn't do something, she was going to be pulled all the way to the other side of the bay where she'd be smashed against the rocks.

Without thinking, I ran over to the lifeguard's hut, grabbed the lifebuoy off the side of the wall and ran as fast as I've ever run in my whole life. Slinging the cord of the lifebuoy round my waist, I dived into the sea and swam so fast it was as though there was a great white shark chasing me.

One, two, three, four, breathe.

One, two, three, four, breathe.

The further out I swam, the colder and rougher the water became. I felt the seawater burn as it went up my nose, but I didn't care. I kicked and kicked my legs until they ached so much that I thought I'd never make it. As I got nearer, I felt my legs being pulled and realised that it was the undercurrent that Mum warned me all about, but I was going to beat it. I saw Alice's head dip under the water and for a second I thought I wouldn't make it. For a moment I thought she was gone for good, but my hands reached out just in time to feel her tiny wrist. I grabbed it tightly and quickly pulled her towards me, looping the lifebuoy round us.

I don't remember the swim back to shore, but the final wave almost threw us both on to the stony beach where I dragged Alice's limp and lifeless body to safety. My heart was pounding so hard that it felt like a deafening drumbeat inside my head. I turned her over and pulled the seaweed away from her face. Her eyes were closed and she wasn't moving at all. *Oh God*, I thought, *she's dead! I didn't make it in time.*

Then I remembered the lifesaving lessons we had at school. As Alice lay there motionless, the lifeguard lesson came back to me. I knew what to do! I had to breathe air into her. I had to give her mouth-to-mouth. I pinched her nose with one hand, leaned over her face quickly and took a deep breath of air, but, as my mouth touched her mouth, she opened her eyes. As my lips touched her lips, she shoved me backwards, sat up quickly, coughing up water and taking big gulps of air, and shouted: 'OH MY GOD, ZACK, DON'T BE SO DISGUSTING!'

I rubbed my eyes and stared.

I wasn't sure what was scarier: the swim, the near-dead Alice or the fact that she was speaking for the first time.

I looked up at her, smiled and said: 'Well, that got you talking.'

And the two of us lay back on the stones and laughed.

21

Alice

Zack Ethan Drake saved my life. He's also the first person I've talked to in ages!

We sat laughing on the stony beach until my feet got pins and needles and I started to get so cold I was shivering. Every time I spoke, Zack smiled and shook his head because it was as though all the words that had been hiding for six months came rattling out of me. I told him everything about me, well, almost everything, and when I said that I was forbidden to go down to Culver Cove he looked surprised.

'Why? It's your beach, isn't it?'

'Yes, but—' Suddenly I felt really sick and I quickly turned over and threw up salty seawater all over him.

'Nice one, Alice. Nicely done. I rescue you and then you chuck up all over me?' But he was smiling when he said it and the way he kind of pulled a face made me laugh a bit.

'Are you OK?' he said as I spat up the last bit of water.

Normally I cry when I'm sick. Usually I go and get Mum, and she rubs my back while I'm sick into the bucket we only ever use for yucky stuff, but this time I didn't. I wiped my mouth with the back of my hand and nodded.

'Will you get in, like, major trouble then?'

'Yes,' I said, standing up. 'Mum and Dad will be really angry with me. You mustn't tell anyone we've been going to the beach. No one can ever know. And I have to get home quick before they notice.'

'Er, you've been away for hours though. They will have noticed by now anyway.'

'Not since the baby got here. They don't care about me any more,' I said angrily, but Zack looked at me like I was really crazy again.

'Don't be an idiot, Alice,' he said, shaking his head. 'Do you really think your mum and dad will have suddenly forgotten all about you because you have a baby sister? What a crazy thing to think.'

I felt the tears in my eyes once more and I just looked up at Zack's puzzled face and nodded.

'Oh my God, that's such a totally crazy thing to think. Mental,' he said, wringing his wet T-shirt out and shaking his head to get the water out of his ears. 'That's like me saying, "Oh, my dad is dead so I'll never think of him again." That would be well stupid, wouldn't it?'

'Yes, but she's their real baby and I'm just . . .' My voice trailed away and I rubbed the tears from my eyes.

'She's a real baby and you're just? Just what? Just stopped talking until now,' he said, laughing. 'Come on, let's walk quicker. I'm getting cold.'

And that's when I started to feel a bit scared again. How was I going to be able to sneak back in without being seen? I'd only ever snuck back into the garden through the door, and I felt my stomach twist up, and my wet clothes felt cold and uncomfortable. My legs felt heavy and tired as though they were full of seawater, but Zack was walking almost two paces faster than me.

'Come on then, chatterbox, we can go back to mine so you can dry off or something.'

I followed him along the top of the stony beach until we reached the harbour wall then I remembered that I'd left my bag at Culver Cove.

'My bag!' I shouted. 'We have to get it!'

'Well, not sure that's a great idea. One almost-drowned Alice is kind of enough for me for one day,' he said, laughing. But when he saw my sad face he stopped smiling and said in a kind voice, 'Don't worry, Alice. We can go back for it tomorrow. It's just a bag.'

But it wasn't just a bag. It had my notebook with the photograph of my other mother tucked inside it. I started to cry.

'But it'll get ruined!' I said, sobbing.

'It's just a bag, Alice. Don't worry.'

'It's not just a bag,' I cried. 'It's not just a bag! My note-book! My photograph!'

I looked up at Zack as the tears rolled down my cheeks. At first he sort of chewed his lip and seemed worried, but then he put an arm round my shoulder and said, 'Don't worry. We can get it back tomorrow, I promise.'

He helped me climb over the wall and as Zack lifted me down on to the path I decided that he was probably the best-est and most brilliant boy in the whole wide world.

Zack's cottage was really pretty. It was just how I imagined it would be, and as I walked up the stairs to the bathroom I hoped that I'd get to come again when I was less wet, soggy and scared.

'Here,' he said, handing me an old-looking T-shirt and a pair of shorts.

The bathroom was tiny, but I loved the little round window above the sink that looked out to sea. I pulled on the dry clothes and looked down at the T-shirt he'd given me. It had a picture of a little yellow plane flying over an island and I remembered what Zack had said about his dad.

As soon as I was changed, I felt better, but as I left the bathroom I noticed a large frame on the wall. It was a picture that was made up of lots and lots of photographs. There was Zack with his dad standing by the little yellow plane. There he was jumping off the back of a big sailing ship with his dad. So many photos of them together: skateboarding, fish-ing, slurping a milkshake, pulling silly faces, playing football. Who would Zack do all of that with now? There was Zack in a funny-looking school uniform, blowing the candles out on his birthday cake, being held as a tiny baby. His dad was in every single picture. Then I noticed one of the dog that Zack had told me all about. Where was it now? I couldn't remember what Zack had said. I stood closer to get a better look and then Zack popped his head round the door.

'What's taking you so long?' he said, but when he saw me looking at the photographs he stopped looking so impatient and sighed. 'That's Otter. He was my dog. Remember I told you about him?' he said, looking sad again.

'Did he die too?'

Zack suddenly looked at me as though I was stupid. 'No, yer div. He's not dead. It's just that Mum reckoned that he should live with some of our friends for a bit. You can't leave Otter on his own for five minutes, and me and Mum are gonna be out loads, so he has to stay with some friends till whenever.'

I must have looked a bit shocked so he carried on. 'We just, like, can't look after him right now. Mum says that when I'm at school and she's at work he'd be alone, and it's not fair to have him shut inside all day all by himself. Actually, I heard her on the telephone one night. She said she thinks it would be better if he always stays at our friend's house though, like a dog adoption thingy.'

He looked really sad when he said that bit and I felt strange too. I wasn't really listening when he showed me his room. I didn't hear what he said when we walked back downstairs, but when he handed me a glass of water I looked up

139

at him and said, 'Do you miss him? Do you want to go back and get him?'

'Of course. Every day. But sometimes I think Mum might be right because who would keep Otter happy when I'm at school? He'd have to be stuck in this tiny place all day and that would suck.'

I couldn't make out most of what Zack said after that because he was eating a banana at the time and he kept spreading peanut butter on it which I thought was gross.

'You want some?' he said when he saw me looking, but I just pulled a face. 'It's good. My dad's favourite thing. It gives you loads of energy too. Here,' he said, holding out a piece of peanutty banana. I slowly put it in my mouth and chewed, but I quickly spat it out.

'Ha!' laughed Zack. 'You either love it or you hate it.' And when he spied the chewed-up food that had landed on his foot he laughed again. 'Er, Alice, I do like you and every-thing, but do you think you could stop spitting up on me?'

We both laughed. 'Actually, that was the other really great thing about Otter. If he was here now, he'd have woofed that chewed-up bit of banana down. Four-legged dustbin, that's what my mum calls him.'

I smiled up at him and I felt even better when Zack said he'd help me sneak back home without being caught.

'Can you draw me a map of your place?' he asked, hand-ing me a clean white sheet of paper. I carefully drew the house, the garden and the lane to the village. He took it from my hands and examined it closely.

'And your dad will still be at work?'

I looked up at the kitchen clock, four twenty exactly, and I nodded quickly.

'Right,' he said, licking the last of the peanut butter off his fingers. 'This is gonna be easy, but you're gonna have to be quick. Go round this side of the house, but duck down behind the wall. That way you won't be seen and you can sneak back in through the side door.' He pointed at the door near our laundry room. 'Well, that's what I'd do anyway. And when you get inside you can get back to your room up the spiral staircase, can't you?'

I smiled. Zack was clever.

As the two of us left the cottage, I spied his skateboard.

'Will you teach me how to do that one time?' I asked.

'Yeah, sure,' he said and we ran over the little stone bridge, past the post office and up the hill. Pippa from the post office shouted after us, but Zack just grabbed my hand and we ran even faster past the churchyard, turning left at the top of the hill on to the little lane to Culver.

'How much further?' Zack said, sounding worried when the lane got narrower and narrower.

'There,' I said, pointing to the top of the hill and the shiny black and gold gates that were just ahead of us.

'This is where you live?' he sort of whispered, looking up at the gates and tracing his finger over the large letters C and M.

'Yes, I've only ever lived here,' I said, wiping the sweat from my forehead.

'My old school had gates a bit like this,' he said, gripping the bars with his hands and resting his cheek on the cold metal. He didn't say else anything for a while and I watched him just stare down the tree-lined driveway where you can see the side of the house and the top of the rose garden wall.

I guess I'd never really stood looking at my home from the gate before. I'd only ever looked from inside out, and it felt kind of strange to be on the outside looking in. It felt sort of horrid and it was a feeling I'd had before. I thought about my sister in the house with my mum, snuggled on the big magical bed, and suddenly it felt peculiar to be outside the gates. The two of us stared like that for a bit when suddenly I heard a car noise. My dad! We ran in through the gates, hid behind the first large oak tree and watched in horror as the car disappeared down the driveway towards the house.

'What do I do now, Zack?' I said, feeling the panic in my new speaking voice.

'You're just gonna have to be mega-quick now. Leg it!'

I watched as the car came to a halt by the garages, but before I turned to run I whispered, 'You mustn't ever tell, Zack, promise?'

'Cross my heart and hope to die,' he said, grinning, and with that I turned and ran.

22

Alice

I ran faster than my little legs have ever run, and when I got to the side of the house I turned back and saw Zack duck out from behind the tree and race back through the gates, so I followed the plan. Crouching down under the windows, I crawled round the house until I reached the stone terrace at the back; now all I had to do was get across it to the side door by the laundry room. Then I heard the sound of Dad's voice. Was he in the garden? If he was, he'd find me before I got inside, before I had a chance to change out of the very big and baggy boy clothes.

'Alice! Alice!'

I heard Dad's voice getting closer and closer and the sound of his shoes crunching on the gravel. I just had to get across the terrace before he saw me. *Crunch, crunch, crunch.*

I peeped out to look and saw him walking up the lawn towards me. He was going to see me, and I felt my heart beat faster and faster, so I did what Zack had told me to do and slid down the wall behind the hedge slowly, slowly, until my whole body was hidden.

'Alice! Where are you?' I could hear his shoes on the stone steps to the terrace: *tip tap toe*; he was getting nearer and nearer, and the sound of my heartbeat throbbed in my ears. I heard him get closer and closer until I saw his feet were about a metre from my face. He tapped his right foot, turned left and headed off back in the opposite direction, away from me, up the garden path. I let out the breath I'd been holding in.

As soon as he was out of sight, I scampered along the terrace to the side door and I think I must have thrown myself at the door because it flung open and I went flying across the red tiled floor of the laundry room. I lay still for a second to be sure I couldn't hear the sound of my mum or my sister with no name. The tiles were cool on my face and my heartbeat slowed, and then I felt myself smiling again. I had made it! I just had time to grab some of my clothes from the pile of washing and get changed, hiding Zack's clothes in the plastic shopping bag and stuffing the bag in the bottom cupboard with all the washing powders.

I slowly walked back into the kitchen and waited. Nothing. Not a single sound, so I grabbed a red apple from the fruit bowl and headed upstairs, feeling very pleased with myself indeed.

With each step, I wondered what I would say to them, now that I could talk again. What should I say first? But when I got to the top of the stairs Mum was sitting at the middle window with the baby and it was, like, stuck to her. She was still wearing her long white nightdress and her hair was piled on top of her head in a large golden bun. I stood watching for a moment; her eyes were closed and the baby, the thing, was sort of sucking on her. As I crept past her, she opened her eyes and smiled at me, but I didn't and I didn't say anything either.

'Alice?' I heard her say as I neared my bedroom. 'Alice? Come here. Would you like to try and hold your little sister? She really wants you to.'

I turned back and for a second I was going to say yes. I opened my mouth to speak, but then Mum rubbed the baby's back like she used to do when I was poorly.

'I'm just trying to get her wind up, Alice. Little babies need you to help them. Would you like to try?'

But I didn't want to. I went into my bedroom and I thought about how happy my mum had looked holding my little sister. I wondered if I ever lay on my other mother's chest like that. Did she hold me at all before I was taken away? As I sat down on the bed, a feeling came over me, around me, above me, until it was as though I was slipping under the water again. I thought about the photograph that I'd left on the beach in my notebook, and for some reason I decided I didn't want it back. For some reason I just wanted to lie down on the bed and close my eyes until the horrid feeling went away.

*   *   *

Mum didn't come down for supper that night because she was too tired. I sat at the kitchen table silently as Dad cooked me some dinner and he told me that my little sister has a thing called colic. He told me colic was when babies get air stuck in their tummies and it can really hurt. He said it made it hard for them to fall asleep and for a moment I felt sorry for the little baby with no name. I felt bad that I hadn't tried to help Mum when she'd asked me. I thought of how Zack had scratched his arms on the harbour wall as he helped me on to the path, and how he hadn't grumbled about it at all. Something felt really wrong. It was as though I knew I needed to do something important, but I couldn't remember what it was.

'You were quite the opposite, Alice,' Dad said suddenly, snapping me out of my miserable thoughts. 'You'd sleep anywhere we took you. Sometimes you were so quiet that Mum and I had to keep checking on you to make sure you were still breathing. The first time we went to Pengarden you slept nearly all the way there and it was Florence, not you, that woke everyone in the castle up every night.'

I loved stories about me as a baby. I sat silently smiling up at him when he told me how they used to call me the Sleeping Beauty Baby. Not like my little sister at all. Who started screaming and crying again at that exact moment and she didn't stop for AGES. Dad told me all about his day at the hospital and the little boy who had stuck playdough up his nose so that he had two enormous green and red nostrils. That almost made me laugh. As he put the plates of food on the table, Dad looked over at my miserable face, reached out his hand and stroked my cheek.

'I hate to see you looking so sad,' he said and I stared down at my plate. 'Alice, I think that you're going to be a brilliant big sister. I think that it would be amazing if you helped Mum and me choose a name for her. What do you think?'

I thought it sounded almost good. I kind of felt like it might be nice. I almost said something.

'Come on then,' he said, picking up the plates, 'let's eat this in front of the TV.' I grinned. Mum doesn't like us to do that, so it was a secret between us.

I felt much better after dinner with Dad. I mean, my ear sort of felt all blocked up with water and my head was hurting a bit, but I didn't mind. I didn't mind that the pasta wasn't really cooked properly or that the sauce didn't taste as nice as when Mum makes it. I was feeling sort of happy and I was going to speak my first words to Dad when he told me that Aunt Aggy, Florence and Casper were coming to stay.

I looked up at him and frowned.

'Alice, come on, don't look like that. You love playing with Florence and they're all so excited to meet your little sister.'

I sat there with my arms folded across my chest and thought about Florence and how she had ignored me the whole time we were at Pengarden. Perhaps I'd just ignore her this time, see how she liked it.

*   *   *

That night I dreamt that I was sleeping in Mum's princess bed, but water came in through the windows and under the door, and it started to fill the room until I was drowning and I couldn't get out. I woke up suddenly. My heart was beating quickly, but the pain that I felt at the side of my head was not in my dream: it was real and more painful than anything I'd ever felt. It was like a red-hot poker was being jabbed inside my ear and when I turned my head the pain shot up the side of my face, along my cheek and behind my eyes. I tried to turn over, but my neck felt stiff, and when I turned the light on the brightness hurt my eyes so badly I had to look away. And it got worse and worse until I couldn't bear it any longer and I was crying and screaming in pain. Until I think I was shouting something.

Dad was the first to come crashing into my room, followed shortly by Mum and the forever-crying baby. When Dad saw my scarlet cheeks and swollen jaw, he put his arm out to stop Mum coming closer.

'Stay there,' he said quietly. 'I'll go and get my bag.'

That's the great thing about having a dad who's a doctor. If you're really ill and in monster pain, he can fix it pretty quickly, and sometimes I just feel better when I see him and his big doctor bag. I heard Dad whisper something into Mum's ear and when he ran back down the hallway Mum sort of backed away from the door.

'I'm so sorry you're hurting, Alice, but Dad is going to make it better.'

I tried to smile, but it hurt the side of my face so much it made me cry instead, and when Dad came back with his bag of magic medicine I heard him tell Mum to take the baby back to the nursery.

Dad looked in my ear and down my throat. He checked my heart, tapped on my back and when he shone a little light in my eyes it hurt so much I had to turn away quickly, but as I did the pain in the side of my head went right down my neck and I fell back on to the pillow. Normally I start to feel better when Dad is there with his bag, but this time I didn't. Instead I started to feel worse and worse and, as I rested my head on the pillow, it felt as though it was being bashed against a pile of rocks.

I didn't have the lovely banana-flavoured medicine or the pink one either. I didn't have a tablet or the fizzy drinking one. This time I had to have an injection and Dad had to hold me still while I wriggled under the covers in agony.

'Alice,' he said softly.

I opened my eyes, but the room looked funny. Everything was getting blurred and smudgy and, when I opened my mouth to speak, my mouth felt dry and sandy. My eyelids closed and the last words I heard were, 'Alice, where have you been?'

23

Zack

Alice Richardson is a chatterbox.

At first it was, like, really weird to hear her speaking. I mean, it was weird when she didn't speak, but I kind of got used to it. Now I'm going to have to get used to the chatter, chatter, chatter. It's not like I don't want to know stuff about her or anything. I mean, for the last two weeks I sort of guessed stuff. I made up an imaginary world that Alice comes from.

After Mum showed me the photograph of the creepy house with its windows all boarded up, I imagined that Alice's world was full of cobwebs, dungeons and scary parents. Before she spoke, I figured that if she didn't talk it was because she was too scared to and perhaps her parents were the sort of monsters that would lock her in the attic if she was bad.

Then, when she told me that her parents could never know she'd been to the beach, I wondered why. It didn't make sense; it wasn't as though she had to swim round the headland to get there. From what she told me, she could just walk out of her garden and down the path, but her parents had told her it was forbidden and that anyway the path was covered in a landslide, but that just wasn't true. Why had they lied to her? If you have one of the world's best beaches practically at the bottom of your garden, why would you not be allowed to go there? I didn't get it.

I had helped Alice get home and was just hiding her wet clothes at the back of the bathroom cupboard when I heard Mum come home from work.

'What have you been up to all day then?' she asked as I walked into the kitchen.

I thought about the nearly-drowned Alice and shrugged my shoulders. 'Nothing much.'

'Nothing?' she said, making a cup of tea. 'And where did you go to do nothing much?'

'Nowhere,' I said, thinking about the black and gold shiny gates of Culver Manor.

'All day?'

'Yeah, pretty much.'

'Hmm,' she said, pouring a ridiculous amount of milk into her mug. 'Well, do you think you might put some suncream on your face next time you go nowhere to spend all day doing "nothing much"?' She kissed my cheek, but

151

didn't say anything else and, after a while, I went back upstairs and tried calling Lou again.

It was weird; we didn't really talk on the phone much when we lived practically round the corner from each other. I mean, he'd, like, call and say, 'I can come over at six' or 'If we pick you up, can your mum collect us from the cinema?' So we never phoned each other to, like, just talk and these days it felt a bit strange. It was as though he didn't know what to say and most of the time I didn't either. The phone rang and rang, and when the answering machine started I sighed, hung up and lay back on the bed.

I started wondering if Alice had made it. I wondered if she'd followed the plan like I'd suggested.

The next morning I was mucking around with my skateboard when Mum left for work.

'Stay out of trouble, please,' she shouted out of the car window and I watched her drive off.

I turned back towards the cottage, heard the chugging noise again and when I looked up the little blue plane was back. I watched it soar higher and higher, and I must have been standing like that for ages when the postman came up behind me. He gave me such a fright I jumped up and fell backwards into the rose bush.

'Sorry,' he said, helping me to my feet. 'Lovely little plane, isn't it? I've been up in it once too.'

'Whose is it?' I asked without thinking.

152

'George Moore. He's a bit of an old eccentric. Lives on the top of Porlock Hill,' he said, pointing to the hill that Mum and I had scrambled up on my first day. 'He collects all sorts of old cars and bikes and that's his little plane. Lovely old boy he is. Everyone loves George.'

I took the pile of post out of his hand, but as I walked back inside the cottage I started to feel a bit sad. I thought about Dad again. I thought about his yellow plane and when I closed my eyes I saw it all again. I saw it falling, falling, and I had to shake my head to stop me seeing any more.

I still hadn't cleaned my teeth when Pippa came over, but my eyes lit up when I saw she had brought two enormous sausage rolls with her.

'Well, I could have brought you one of my world-famous, hideous sandwiches on slightly mouldy bread, but I think these are just the ticket for a hungry boy.'

'You eat mouldy sandwiches?' I said, looking up at her.

'Oh well, it has been known. That's what happens if you try and make lunch without putting your glasses on.'

I inspected the sausage rolls for signs of mould.

'You friends with that Alice then?' she suddenly said. When I didn't reply, she said, 'I saw you with her yesterday. Are you friends? Does she talk to you?'

I still didn't say anything because I really didn't want to get Alice in trouble and, after a while, she gave up and made herself a cup of tea and I stuffed the lovely warm pastry in my mouth.

Later that day, I scrambled over the last boulder to Culver Cove, but Alice wasn't on the beach. I hoped she was OK.

When she wasn't there the day after that, I started to imagine that maybe she hadn't made it back to the house in time. I imagined she'd been caught just as she got to the door and was now locked in the attic where she would spend the rest of the summer. On the third day of her being missing I was just drying off from a swim when I saw a pink thing out of the corner of my eye. The bag! I'd totally forgotten I'd promised Alice I'd get it back for her. I suddenly felt really bad that I'd forgotten. Luckily, it hadn't rained the whole week.

I walked over to the bag and picked it up and that's when I realised that being on the beach wasn't as much fun without Alice. I mean, even though she's a girl and even though she's too scared to swim with the seals, it was kind of better with her. Bodyboarding was more fun when there was someone there to laugh or cheer you along.

Alice reminds me a bit of Lou because she always seems to want to do something a bit silly to make me laugh. She does these really funny animal walks that are made up of two different animals. It's a bit like charades and I have to guess which end of her is what animal. I don't know why it's funny, but it is. I think the chicken shark was the one that made me sort of laugh all day. It makes me smile just thinking about it.

I put the bag on my shoulder and decided to head home, when something caught my eye. A shape at the far end of the beach. No, not a shape, a person. A person who was not Alice. It was a man. I saw him wave and start running towards me. My feet sank into the sand and my heart began to beat faster. I thought about the 'Private property. Keep out' sign and my stomach flipped over a bit like when you drive over a bridge really fast. I was *so* in for it now. I looked at the water, but the tide was still really high. My heart started beating faster and faster. How could I get off the beach now? I didn't want to do the scary swim round the headland. I never wanted to swim that far out again after what nearly happened to Alice.

The man came closer and I heard him shout out. I knew I had to do something, but I was trapped. What if that was Alice's scary dad? What would he do? Would he grab me and drag me back up the beach? What do they do to people who trespass on their special beach? I turned to look back at the water, but there was no way I wanted to try swimming out there again. I looked back up towards the man; he was getting closer and closer. I had no choice. There was nothing else I could do; there was nowhere I could run; so I turned round and, even though the tide was as high as I have ever seen it, I started to wade into the sea.

24

Zack

'No!' shouted the man, but I carried on.

'Please don't!' I heard him shout again. 'Please!'

Something in his voice told me he wasn't angry. I stopped just as the water reached my knees and when I turned back the man was racing down the beach towards me. I watched him slowly walk over to me and I could see that he had the sort of hair that isn't really red like Lexi's, but it isn't really blonde either, and he was probably one of the tallest men I had ever seen. I felt afraid, but as he got closer he smiled. When he saw my frightened face, he crouched down and spoke in the softest, kindest voice.

'I'm David. I'm Alice's dad. You're not in any trouble, but please don't swim round the headland. It's too dangerous.' He held out a freckly hand to me and I told him my name.

He was nothing like I'd imagined at all. He wasn't, you know, some kind of horrid ogre dad like I thought he might be. He was really nice and he wasn't mad at all.

'Those "Keep out" signs were put there a long time ago by my father,' he said, pointing out towards the boulder, and I felt a little shudder ripple down my spine. 'My father thought it would be better to stop anyone trying to come here from the other side in case somebody from the village drowned.'

I thought about Alice and my heart skipped a beat. He looked at me with squinty eyes and then he smiled. I waded back towards the shore.

'I haven't been down here for years,' he said, resting his back against one of the two boulders that looked like pillars. 'I forgot how beautiful it is.' He reached out a hand towards me. 'I'll take Alice's bag, shall I? Not sure I'd have wanted to have been seen with a pink Barbie bag when I was your age. Unless this is actually your bag of course?'

I laughed. 'Er, that's a no.'

'Didn't think so. Hmm,' he said, looking at the picture on the front of the bag, 'I'll never understand why girls like this sort of thing.'

'Me neither,' I said, laughing. 'My friend Lexi has a bedroom that is literally pink times four hundred.'

'Ha! That's good. Well, I don't know about you, Zack, but I'm hungry times four hundred so let's head back up the safe way. Let's get you home.'

I followed him towards the waterfall, but all I could think about was whether he would tell Mum.

'I hear you've moved here from London.'

I didn't say anything.

'I went to university in London. Great place to live, but it's pretty good down here too. Zack,' he said slowly, 'is there anything you think you should tell me?'

I felt my cheeks get hot and I looked down at the sand.

'If I was your age,' he said, putting the rucksack on his shoulder, 'and had just moved here, I might just go off exploring too, Zack.'

I kind of smiled, looked up at him and decided that Alice must have told her parents all about me in her new chatter-box voice, but I was wrong. Dr Richardson had heard all about me and Alice from Pippa when he'd been to the post office that morning, but he didn't know everything.

We went back to Culver Manor along the path and even though I'm not really scared of heights or anything like that I felt really dizzy when I looked down the waterfall. When I saw the ledge that Alice had had to jump over every time she came down, I was really impressed that she'd made it. Alice might not have wanted to get too close to the seals, but she was brave enough to do that scary jump every time.

At the door Dr Richardson stopped. 'Are you sure there's nothing you want to tell me?' he asked me again. 'I won't be cross.'

I shook my head. I felt myself get nervous. *Maybe I should tell him*, I thought. *Perhaps it won't matter*. But then I remembered that I had promised Alice, and Dad always said you should never, ever break your promises.

We walked through the garden side by side, but I wasn't really paying attention to anything, and when we got to the driveway Dr Richardson put the little rucksack down and sighed. 'Zack, you're not in any trouble, but there's something you should know. It's about Alice.'

I listened quietly and looked down at the ground. Poor Alice. I didn't dare look up in case I blurted it out. I was bound to get the blame. If they knew that Alice had followed me, if they knew she'd copied me, I'd be in more trouble than I'd ever been in my whole entire life. As I listened to what had happened to Alice the night she'd been rescued, I felt worse than ever. I stared at the tops of my trainers and bit down hard on my lip. I stood like that for ages and when I didn't say a word Dr Richardson looked down at me hopefully.

'Well, you'd best get home, Zack,' he said. But as I turned to leave he shouted, 'Say hi to your mum, won't you?'

Mum got home about five minutes after me and I came downstairs slowly to say hello. I don't know why, but I felt like the only thing I wanted was a hug from her or something.

'Well, that's a lovely way to be greeted,' she said as I squeezed her tightly. 'It's like having old Zack back again.' I looked at her face and noticed a red mark across her cheek.

'What's that?' I asked, touching the red mark which felt swollen under my fingers.

'Oh, that's your mother trying to do everything in time for yesterday as usual. I was standing on a chair to get some art supplies down from a cupboard and managed to knock a plastic storage box on top of me. Don't worry, it doesn't hurt. It was more embarrassing than anything because the whole of the staffroom saw,' she said, laughing, and I squeezed her even more tightly.

That night I got my guitar out from under my bed and we did something we hadn't done since Dad died. I sat on the sofa next to Mum and I played and played as she sang one of her favourite songs. That's the weird thing about my mum. She's short and sort of spiky, but she has the softest, loveliest singing voice that you ever heard. It made me think of what Dad had told me.

'The first time I saw your mum she was sitting cross-legged and playing the guitar. Every girl in the room disappeared when I saw her. All my worries stopped being worries when I heard her sing.'

And he was right. All my worries stopped feeling horrid for a while. I forgot the sad news about Alice I had heard from Dr Richardson. There was a happy, warm feeling in the house until the phone rang. Mum took the call and when she was finished she looked at me with angry, scary eyes that were filled with tears.

'What the hell have you been up to?' she shouted.

Everything was fine until it wasn't.

25

Zack

'You've got some explaining to do!' she said, but I didn't look up. 'That was David Richardson on the phone. I knew something funny was going on with you. Well? What have you got to say for yourself?' Her voice got louder and louder, but I didn't know what to say. 'I told you about staying away from that beach. I specifically told you not to go there. I made it absolutely clear, didn't I?'

That's when I realised she was actually upset. She wasn't just angry; she had eyes that were filled with tears too.

'Poor Alice,' she kept saying over and over again. 'Poor David.' She sighed and looked at me. 'Zack? Why?'

I didn't say a thing, but as she closed the curtains above the television I noticed the blue flashing lights of a police car by the Boathouse Café.

'Zack, will you just answer me, please?' She sounded angrier now and when I did finally look up at her she was shaking with rage. I didn't dare say a word; all I could think about was Alice. She'd seemed fine when I last saw her. She looked perfectly OK as I watched her running down the driveway and when David had told me what had happened I was hoping it would all just go away. Why had he telephoned my mum? My mind drifted back to Alice's lifeless body as I'd dragged it up the beach. I remembered the relief I'd felt when she came back to life. *Poor Alice*, that's what Mum had said . . . what if?

I think Mum had been shouting some more, but I'd been so busy thinking about Alice that I hadn't heard her. She came round the coffee table so that she was standing in front of me.

'Zack!' she bellowed. 'Are you listening to me at all? Do you know how lucky you are to still be alive? Have I not been through enough without you risking your life just to go for a stupid swim?'

I thought about Dad and his jumping-out-of-planes job. I thought of how Dad was always risking his life until he risked it a bit too much and I felt angry.

'Dad did!' I shouted back. 'That's what he did every day, wasn't it?' I said, feeling my throat get tight and doing my best to stop myself from crying. 'How can you have a go at me for just going to some stupid beach when Dad did crazy things all the time?' I screamed at her. I almost spat the words out and the anger started to rise up in me until I was screaming terrible things at her, until I was shouting the worst and most horrid words back at her, until I was shaking as much as she had been. Until I lifted the guitar up into the air and, without thinking, I smashed it down hard over the television.

Splinters of wood flew across the room and the strings twanged backwards at my face. I felt one scratch my left cheek, but I wasn't finished yet. I threw what was left of the guitar across the room and then I kicked the table over.

'Zack! Stop!' Mum shouted, but with my left hand I swept all the photographs off the mantelpiece.

'Zack! Please stop!' she cried out, but I picked up a mug and threw that against the wall. I couldn't hear anything any more, just a sort of humming, buzzing sound, but as I kicked the log basket over Mum had to leap out of the way, falling backwards over the kicked-over table. With my hand, I grabbed the vase from the window sill and I was just about to throw it at the kitchen door when there was a loud knock at our front door.

Bang! Bang! Bang!

Mum lay in a crumpled heap on the floor. I stopped shouting, the vase still raised above my head.

Bang! Bang! Bang!

I felt my chest rise and fall with each breath.

'Open the door!' a man's deep voice called out. 'Open the door now! It's the police!'

I saw Mum wipe the tears from her cheeks and the shock of what I'd done began to creep upwards from my feet. Upwards and upwards, like dark shadowy fingers that moved higher towards my chest. Tighter and tighter I felt them grip my shoulders until the door was flung open and two policemen came barging into our little cottage.

Mum didn't move and neither did I. I watched the policemen's faces as they looked around at the room. I saw them eye the broken furniture, the shattered glass, the smashed-up bit of guitar and the look of fear on Mum's face.

'You!' said the smaller of the two policemen, pointing at me. 'You stay right there.'

I felt my heart thumping in my chest; the buzzing, humming noise began to fade. Out of the corner of my eye I saw my mum get to her feet and I wanted to die. But when the younger policeman saw the red mark on her face he turned to me.

'Did you do that?' he asked, looking disgusted. I looked over at Mum and then back at the policeman.

I saw him reach for his handcuffs and I panicked. I heard Mum say, 'No, no, he didn't do that.' She said angrily, 'Don't be crazy! He didn't touch me. I had an accident at work. Really, we're fine.'

I could see they didn't believe her. The smaller policeman shook his head and they both moved closer.

'We heard the noise coming from this house. It seems like we got here just in time,' he said, stepping over the shards of glass towards me.

I saw the open door and didn't think. I just ran. I ran out of the door and over the bridge, up the lane and past the café. I ran until I felt the sweat dripping down my back and

164

a stitch in my side, but the sound of police sirens got louder. I ran through the churchyard where my grandfather was buried and I didn't stop. I leapt over the wall to the lane, grazing the backs of my legs as I fell forward. I made a dash through someone's garden and a security light flashed on as I collided with a bin. I jumped over a rose bush, taking half the petals with me and catching the thorns against my arms. I ran until my legs were almost falling forward by themselves and my lungs burned so much I thought I couldn't take it any more.

I turned left in the village at a sign I recognised, but the streetlights disappeared and darkness surrounded me. I ran further and further, the sirens seemed to fade and I had only moonlight to guide my way. The road became a lane, the lane became a track and the track became a scramble. I was running and then I wasn't. I was scrambling up a track and then I wasn't. I stood at the beacon on Porlock Hill, where I'd been with my mother on that first day and I looked down the moonlit vale and out towards the black-ened sea.

Everything was fine until it wasn't, and I knew right then that I couldn't run any more.

I waited until I got my breath back and felt my racing heartbeat become normal again. Then, with shaking legs and aching arms, I turned round to face the journey home. But which way? In front of me were two paths. Which one was the way back down? I didn't know, so I just guessed and headed left along a path, hoping that I'd picked correctly.

I was wrong. I think I must have been slowly walking for twenty minutes or so when I realised it wasn't right, but something told me to keep going. Even though I knew in my heart it was the wrong way, I kept going and going until the sweat on my skin made me feel cold and shivery. I think I was almost sleepwalking when I saw a building in the distance. A sort of house that seem to shine. Was it made of glass? I couldn't be sure. Did I see my face reflected in the walls? I was too tired to think or care and I stumbled round the building to ask for help. I cried out, but no one came.

My teeth were chattering so much I could feel the vibration in my head, but there was no sign of life in the house. I wandered round the back of the shiny building until I saw what looked like a barn or was it bigger? It could have been stables, but I didn't hear any horses and I sighed with such relief when I saw a door was open. I stepped inside.

I reached up on the wall and felt for a light switch which clicked loudly as I turned it on. The lights flickered slowly on and off; a strange humming noise echoed off the walls. The lights continued to flicker as though they couldn't decide whether to work or not and then suddenly the room was lit up. I expected sleeping cows or horses. I imagined the smell of hay or the sight of riding boots lined up against a wall. I thought there'd be a rusting tractor, a sleeping sheep-dog or a lawnmower. I expected all of these, but that's not what I saw.

I blinked once. I blinked twice and I almost pinched my arm to make sure I wasn't imagining it. I was in a huge room which contained a collection of the most amazing things. An old motorbike and sidecar, a shiny red Ferrari, its bonnet freshly polished, two Aston Martins and my favourite ever car, a 1957 Mercedes-Benz Gullwing. How had Dad described it? A thing of beauty? And in the middle of the room was a plane. I smiled. It was the little blue plane that I kept seeing. It had to be the same one.

I felt myself being sort of pulled over to it and before I knew what I was doing I was staring at my own reflection in the door. Was it open? I reached up with my left hand. *Click, click*. It was locked. I walked round the plane and sighed. It was the same one as Dad's. A Tiger Moth. I felt my eyes start to close. I was so tired. I looked around for somewhere to rest my aching body, but the concrete floor was uninviting. I tried the Gullwing first, but it was locked, then the Ferrari, but it was as well. I tried both the Astons and then a little silver Porsche and in the end I spied a dark green car I didn't need to worry about locks for because it didn't have a roof.

I ran back to the door to switch off the lights and crept back to the corner of the room. A Rolls-Royce. It had to be one of the oldest cars I'd ever seen, and I took my shoes off before I carefully climbed over the door and on to the spring-iest leather seats I'd ever sat on. I felt my eyelids closing and I lay back on the creamy white seats and fell fast asleep.

26

Zack

I woke up slowly and a woollen blanket tickled my nose. I tried to move. Everything hurt. I turned my head and my neck felt stiff and painful. Something wasn't right. This wasn't my bed and I suddenly remembered the night before. *The night before. Oh God*, I thought. *What have I done?*

I looked up at the ceiling. A tiny bird flew up into the roof and, as I turned my head to watch it disappear into a nest, I saw a man standing by the car. His hair was almost white; it curled upwards and outwards in a way that made me think that the red baseball cap he was wearing was there to keep it from springing away. He leaned against the bonnet of the Rolls-Royce and looked back at the little plane. I watched him take a puff of his pipe; a plume of bluish smoke hovered round his face and then he turned to me and smiled.

'Well, I guess if I had to pick a car to fall asleep in I'd have chosen the Roller too.' He rested a hand on the door of the car and looked right at me. I peered back at him over the woollen blanket. His face was tanned and papery-looking and there were long creases along his forehead, and around his mouth and eyes. He wore a greenish shirt with the collar turned right up and I noticed that there were tiny holes and rips and stains all over it. He looked down at his shirt. 'I hate wearing overalls to work in. I think I've had this polo shirt since little Nelly died.'

'Who was little Nelly?' I asked, folding the blanket away from my face, but the old man just laughed.

'Ha! It's just something my father used to say. No idea who she was, but I've no idea who you are either,' he said, stroking the side of his face.

I took one more look round the room at the collection and sighed when I saw the plane. I thought of the night before and a horrible feeling of dread came over me. *What's going to happen to me? Mum*, I thought and I saw her frightened face as the police had come barging into the house. *Did they really think I'd hurt my own mum? Were they still looking for me?* I was going to get into so much trouble. I felt the scratch on my cheek. I thought about my smashed-up guitar and I wanted to crawl into a hole and never come out.

'You look like you've got the weight of the world on your shoulders,' said the man and I did. It felt as though everything was piling on top of me. 'I'm George,' he said, opening

169

the door for me and, as I lifted my aching legs out of the car, I looked at him.

'I'm Zack.'

I followed him back across the room, but I slowed down when we reached the wings of the plane.

'A Tiger Moth,' I said, reaching out and touching the tip of one wing.

George looked at me in surprise. 'Beautiful, isn't she?'

I nodded. 'My dad's was yellow.'

'Did he fly it much?'

I nodded again, but then I pressed my thumb on the side of the wing and winced in pain.

'Oh crikey!' said George, looking at the red and swollen thumb. 'That's quite a splinter you've got there. Let's go inside and I'll get it out for you, but then, young man,' he said, ruffling the top of my hair, 'then we'd best get you home.'

Home, I thought. What was waiting for me there?

We walked round the side of the building I had stumbled round the night before and as we turned left to the house I looked up in amazement. It was a house like I had never seen before. I hadn't imagined it. It *was* shiny; I *had* seen my face reflected in the walls because it was a house that was made entirely of glass. A sort of glass box which shimmered in the sunlight.

'Come on then,' said George, holding open the door, and I stepped inside.

It was a room a bit like the one in my old house where the kitchen, the sitting room and the place where you eat are all in one room, and in the middle a kind of fireplace hung down from the ceiling so that you could walk all the way round it. At one side of the room was a fish tank, but it was the size of the ones you see at the aquarium. I saw three black, orange and white fish swim by as I walked past it.

'So,' said George as he held my thumb carefully under the light, 'you look like you've been in the wars. Bad night, huh?' he asked, but I said nothing. I winced as he tried to free the splinter from underneath the skin. 'Let me guess, you had a row with your mum and dad, you said things you wish you hadn't and now you need to lick your wounds, eh?' Still I said nothing. 'Or did you do something you really shouldn't have and instead of taking the punishment you ran off?'

I watched with relief as the largest splinter I'd ever seen was prised out of my swollen thumb. 'Things are never that bad, you know,' he said, wiping the wound with a bit of cotton wool that made it sting.

I didn't say anything, but a photograph on the wall behind his head caught my eye. It was a picture of the car that I'd slept in and sitting on the back seats was a group of children that I recognised. My mum sat squashed in between two boys and in the front seat, with her arms in the air, was a girl with long blonde hair; she was sitting on the lap of the boy who peeped out from behind my granddad in the other photo. Where had I seen that smile before? It was there in my mind, but I couldn't tease it out of my head.

When George saw me staring at the photo, he sighed. 'My wife called that lot the Famous Five, you know, like the books.' I waited for him to tell me more, but he didn't and on hearing my stomach rumble louder than it ever had he smiled and handed me a biscuit.

'Right, young Zack, there's one thing I know for sure: your parents will be very worried about you so why don't we go and choose a car and I'll drive you home.'

I chose the Ferrari. We drove back down the hill with the roof down and it made me think of that last day with Dad. When I pointed out my home to George, he went quiet. 'You live here?' he said slowly.

I unbuckled my seat belt and nodded. 'We just moved here. It used to be my granddad's cottage, but—'

George suddenly looked upset. I saw his hands grip the steering wheel so hard they went sort of white. 'Are you Jane's son?'

I nodded and when I looked into his eyes I saw they were filled with tears. He turned away and coughed. 'Time to face the music,' he said, without turning back to me. 'Off you go.'

I thought about the smashed-up guitar, about the police and about Alice. I felt the panic rising and for a moment I wanted to stay put. For a second I thought about telling him or asking him to take me into town.

As if George could read my mind, he turned back to my frightened face, put a hand on my shoulder and said, 'Nothing is ever as bad as it seems.' But I saw a tear roll down his cheek.

I climbed out of the car slowly, thanking George as I shut the door. I watched him drive back up the road. What had made him so sad I wondered? I was just standing on the road like that for ages, my head full of questions, when the door to the cottage was suddenly flung open. Mum came running out towards me, her arms outstretched, and I could see her eyes were puffy and red.

'Zack!' she said, throwing her arms round me. 'My Zack! Where have you been?'

'I'm sorry,' I said quietly. 'I'm so sorry.'

She bent down towards me; her eyes were filled with tears and she kissed me on my forehead, my cheeks and then my nose. 'I was so worried about you.'

When we went inside, I saw that Mum had already cleared up the mess from the night before. The police, Mum told me as we tucked into bacon sandwiches, were across the street last night, investigating a suspected burglary, when they heard the shouting from our cottage. She had explained to them about Dad and everything else and they'd understood.

'But they were chasing me in their car,' I said worriedly.

'No they weren't, sweetheart. Just after you legged it, they got a call about an emergency in town.'

I thought about the police sirens I'd heard and I felt kind of stupid. I thought about the guitar and the sound of breaking glass and I felt horrid. 'I'm sorry,' I said again.

'It's OK. Well, it's not OK to lose your temper like that, it really isn't, but you have had a lot to cope with this last year. We both have. Shall we try starting again?'

I smiled and nodded.

'Are you going to tell me where you went last night?' I took a bite out of my sandwich, a slurp of my Diet Coke and I told her the whole story, but when I was finished she just stared.

'You found your way to George's house? All that way? Of all the places you could have ended up!'

But when I told her I'd fallen asleep on the back seat of a dark green Rolls-Royce she made a little yelping sound and put her hands to her face and slowly shook her head. I remembered the photograph I'd seen.

'George said you were one of a sort of Famous Five. Is that—'

Mum suddenly looked up at me with worried eyes. 'He said that?' She set down her mug of tea, leaned in closer and said very quickly, 'What else did he say? What else did he tell you?' She looked afraid; her eyes were wide and alert. 'Well?' she said more insistently.

'N . . . nothing,' I sort of stammered. 'He didn't say anything else. Why, what would he have said?'

She got up from the table and went into the kitchen, so I followed her.

'What is it?' I asked as I watched her move round the kitchen, picking things up and putting them back down again. She leaned against the back door and sighed. She rubbed her eyes, kneaded her temples and frantically twirled her wedding ring round and round.

'When I was . . . when David, Aggy and I were younger, we . . .' She turned her back to me and stared out of the back

174

door window and across the stony beach. I waited and waited, but she didn't finish her sentence. What was going on?

'Mum?' I stared at the back of her head and I thought I heard her muttering something under her breath. Did she say kimmen or killen? I couldn't be sure.

She let out a long deep breath, turned to face me and in a sort of high-pitched, weird voice she said, 'Alice, we have to think about Alice.' Then she explained to me what Dr Richardson had told her on the phone and I felt sad. They just thought that Alice had snuck down to the beach and been for a swim. They didn't know the truth and the truth was beginning to feel like a secret I shouldn't be keeping any more.

27

Alice

I think my name is Alice, but I don't know where I am.

It feels like I'm asleep, but I don't think that I'm dreaming.

It feels like I'm floating, but I don't think I'm in the sea.

I think I hear birds singing and the distant sound of waves.

I know I'm sort of somewhere, but I don't know where here is. Sometimes I see a beach and a garden with white walls. I think I wandered down a lane with trees as tall as tall. I was sitting in a room; the floor was pinkish white and all the while the windows were lit with blue moonlight. Sometimes I think I see my mum. Or is it someone else I see?

I think I can hear some voices, but I don't know who they are. I saw a boy with the darkest hair; he was near. He was far.

I think I saw a woman; her dress was whitest white. I don't know where I am, if it's day or if it's night.

I once thought I heard a crying sound, but it was far away. It kept coming and going then it stopped one day.

It feels like I'm flying, but I know I'm on the ground. There's something soft beneath me, but it isn't sand I feel. Sometimes I think I see a woman; she has golden hair. She sparkles in the sunlight; her skin is fairest fair. She makes me think of lilac roses, reddest velvet and lemon cake. I don't know if I'm sleeping or if I'm wide awake.

It feels like I am dreaming, but something here is different. I hear the voices louder now and one of them is Dad. I almost see his hair and the freckles on his hands; it makes me think of medicine and splashing in the bath. I hear them talking louder now, but no one seems to laugh.

I'm trying to move, but I just can't free my body. It feels like I really want to, I just have to remember how.

I hear something beeping, but I don't know what it is. I feel a scratch on my skin, fast footsteps on the floor.

I feel a hand on my hand and it strokes me gently.

I feel lips on my cheek as she kisses me softly.

And then I don't feel anything.

28

Zack

Dr Richardson is Alice's dad, but he says I can call him David.

I wandered outside slowly; it was already almost the hottest day ever, and I was sticky and sweaty by the time I reached the shiny black and gold gates of Culver Manor. I pulled the map out of my pocket and followed David's instructions to meet him by the large cedar tree at the bottom of the south lawn, but as I ran down the winding driveway I heard the chugging noise and I looked up at the sky. There was the little blue plane. I wondered where George was going.

The lawn sloped away from the house and I looked towards the grey stone of the house up to the three large windows. The garden was kind of made up of lots of different bits, with a place that just had lots of roses and one with only fruit trees, but I knew I was going to love the part of the garden where the big cedar tree was most.

I saw David standing by the tree and, when he saw me looking around at all the different coloured flowers which sort of smelt a bit like perfume but nice, he waved at me to come over to him.

'You like it?'

I nodded.

'I know it's not the sort of thing that boys can get too excited about, but my wife made this part of the garden and I think it looks a bit like a painting, don't you?'

I did; he was right. It did look like the sort of painting I'd seen at that gallery my mum had dragged me round.

'Now, young man,' he said, handing me a pair of gloves, 'we have a lot to do and if we work really hard it'll be ready just in time.'

We worked all that day and it was hot and sweaty work, but I loved it. On the second day Alice's dad met me in the garden with a glass of juice and told me he had to go back to the hospital to see her.

'Will Alice be . . . I mean, will she . . .' My voice trailed off and I had to stop myself from blurting it all out, but when I looked up again David looked so sad that I clenched my mouth shut.

'I hope so, Zack. We just have to be patient. She's in the best place to be looked after. Besides,' he said more cheerily, 'she'll have something waiting for her, won't she?'

I watched him walk back up the lawn to the terrace and my heart sank deeper and deeper. I wanted to run after him and tell him that it was my fault. I wanted to tell him that Alice hadn't just been for a swim: she'd tried to swim round the headland because of me. I wanted to tell him the reason she was so ill was my entire fault. But I was frozen still.

On the third day I met Alice's mum for the first time. I guess I expected her to look like the woman in the photograph Alice had. I mean, I look just like my dad and, because my mum is always changing her hair colour, no one would know that my thick black hair is just like hers. Mum once said that, when I was born, Dad kissed me and left his smile behind because sometimes, when I laugh at something, or smile at her, she holds out her hand, touches my cheek and says: 'You're the best thing we ever did, Zack.'

'I'm Sophie,' Alice's mum said, handing me a plate of delicious-looking sandwiches, an apple, a slice of cake and a bottle of squash. Her hair was sort of tied in a plait that hung all the way down her back and she spoke in a voice that was so soft I could hardly hear her. She's much taller than my mum and she sort of moves as though she's kind of floating above the grass, not like Mum who sort of stomps very quickly as though she has to get everywhere like yesterday. 'You're doing a brilliant job, Zack,' she said, but then the baby started crying, and she smiled at me and went back up to the house.

I don't know what the baby is called, but it is, like, so loud. I mean, it's not like I haven't been around babies

before, but this one does not stop screaming and
I wondered how anything so small could be so n
anyone ever got any sleep in this house. If I cou
the bottom of the garden, you must be able to he
walls too.

That night, when me and Mum were watching telly, I saw
her twirl a strand of her now red hair round her finger and
it made me think of Sophie.

'Alice doesn't really look like her mum or her dad. It's
weird; she doesn't really look like she's from the same family
at all.'

My mum looked at me. 'Alice is adopted. Sophie and
David aren't her birth parents. But you mustn't ask Alice
about that, Zack; it's not the sort of thing you ask
someone.'

That night I fell asleep really quickly and I dreamt that I was
running along the stony beach with Otter and Alice, so in
the morning I asked Mum when we could get him back, but
she just shook her head. It made me feel sort of angry. I kept
thinking that if Otter stayed at Lexi's for too long he'd probably forget all about me too.

So when I went to Culver Manor that day I was in a bad
mood. Walking through the gates made my mood worse as I
thought of my old school, and all my friends there, and
about the new school I'd be going to soon and a cold sensation came trickling down my spine. I wandered down the

…eway slowly, as though my legs had forgotten how to work properly. It was like I didn't want to be here or there or anywhere. I must have been standing like that, just staring, when I heard my name. I looked up and saw David standing at the front door.

'Over here, Zack!' he shouted and I followed him through the grey stone archway beyond the ancient wooden door and into Culver Manor for the very first time.

29

Alice

My name is Alice Richardson and I think I am here now.

Sometimes I get so hot it feels as though my eyes are burning and my whole body gets so warm the sheets are wet with sweat. Sometimes I feel so cold that my teeth chatter and my body shakes. Last night I woke up freezing. I was freezing, freezing cold. Mum and Dad lifted me up together and I heard her voice again. She laid me in a warm bath and it felt like my skin was melting. I looked up at her pale face; I felt her arm round my shoulders and a warm sponge on my arms.

'Poor baby,' she kept saying, 'my poor baby.'

She cradled me in the water until I felt the tingle of life come back to my body.

I know I've been asleep, but I don't know for how long. I think I'm at home now, but something here is wrong. I think

I saw my dad; he smiled and stroked my cheek. I heard his voice, but he was speaking to someone else. I heard him say they were making it for me. I heard him say I needed to get better. I heard him say that it was so hot outside that I couldn't miss any of the summer.

He asked me where I'd been, what I'd done, who I'd seen. I heard him say a name I knew.

I am so tired. I have tried to sit up, but it just feels too hard.

Tomorrow I'll try harder, but for now I'll rest again while my mum watches me, a little baby asleep on her chest.

30

Zack

Alice Richardson has the most amazing house I have ever been in. She has to get better.

Today David showed me all round the downstairs of Culver Manor and it is massive. It's even bigger than it looks. The hallway is a bit like a church and is so big you could totally play football in there, which is what David said him and his big brother used to do, until they smashed one of the special windows above the door. He showed me the library which has bookcases that go up as far as the ceiling and stretch the length of both the end walls where a tiny ladder rests against the shelves. At the far end are two arched windows and a large wooden desk with a dark green leather top sits perfectly between them.

'That was my father's desk,' he said and I noticed the leather was curling at the edges and there were marks where a pen had pressed too hard against paper so that an impression of someone's handwriting was left behind.

'My brother got into big trouble for that,' he said, sort of laughing and tracing his finger along the marks that were scored into the leather.

The end wall was covered in a map. A map of the coast and its faded blue sea was dotted with names I didn't recognise.

'The south-west,' David said when he saw me peering up at it. 'That's the south-west coastline from Bristol down to St Ives in Cornwall,' and he pointed to the very tip.

'Dad took me to Cornwall once,' I said without thinking. 'We went surfing there together, but I wasn't much good,' I told him and I remembered how I couldn't even lift my body up on to the board until the very last day and even then I kept falling off.

Bodyboarding was much easier. Even Alice could do that. She was really good. She'd got the hang of it pretty quickly and even when a wave had dunked her into the sand she didn't moan or anything like I'd done the first time it had happened to me. Even when the salty seawater had burned her nose and she got a bit of sand in her eyes, she didn't complain. She just sort of got on with it. She just shook the water out of her ears, stood up and tried again. Poor Alice; thinking about her made me feel sad once more.

'Takes practice,' David said, looking down at my miserable face. 'You'll get better.'

I followed him back into the garden where we spent all day building the special thing for Alice, but every time I looked up and out to sea I thought about how Dad wasn't here to show me things any more. So David was wrong: how would I get better at anything without Dad to teach me?

Later that day I wandered back down the lane to our cottage slowly and the sad feeling that started at Culver Manor wouldn't go away. I didn't say much when I got home, but Mum was doing that thing where she asks me tons of questions about really stupid things and in the end I went upstairs to bed early. I fell asleep in my clothes and it was Mum's singing that sort of woke me up. She was tiptoeing round my bedroom, tidying things up.

'Not much point creeping around if you're gonna sing, Mum,' I said, but I didn't really mind.

When I was younger, and went to the little school, I used to find it really hard to get up early in the mornings, especially when it was winter and it was still dark outside. But my mum had a way of waking me up that made it less horrid. She would come into my bedroom and start singing really softly so that I'd always wake up to the sound of her lovely voice.

She turned round and smiled back at me.

'Mum,' I said slowly. 'How come we never came here before?'

Mum stopped smiling then and a dark shadow appeared across her face. She sat down slowly on the edge of my bed and sighed. 'I think it's time I told you the truth about the beach and what happened there.'

I felt my heart beat quickly and I sort of held my breath as I waited for Mum to tell me more, but then the telephone rang and Mum got up from the bed and went downstairs.

'How lovely to hear from you,' I heard her say.

There was a silence and then I heard her try to speak quietly which is kind of hard for Mum because she only has two volume settings: loud and louder.

'I was just thinking about him,' she sort of whispered and then I heard a little cry. 'I really miss him,' she said over and over again, and I guessed she must be talking to Hannah. They often have really long phone calls when Mum talks about Dad and cries a lot; usually it's late at night when Mum thinks I'm asleep.

'What a good idea,' I heard Mum say, sounding happier. 'What a lovely thing to suggest. It would be really lovely to see you again. What's it been, twenty-five years?'

Twenty-five years? What was she talking about? We saw Hannah just last month. It didn't make sense.

'You're right. That's so kind of you. Zack really needs to try again and if it doesn't work this time we can keep trying. Get back in the saddle and all that.'

Trying what? What was a good idea? What was she talking about? Who was she talking to? A saddle? But I didn't even have a bike any more. Perhaps I was going to *get* a bike?

Then Mum's voice went really quiet and I couldn't hear her any more. I tried to stay awake because I really wanted to know what the phone call was about, and what she'd been going to tell me about Culver Cove, but my eyes were too heavy and I drifted off to sleep.

The next morning was cloudy and kind of misty. I went to Culver Manor again, but I hadn't long been in the garden when it started to rain. It was the sort of big splashy rain that you sometimes get in really hot countries. It started suddenly as though a rain switch had just been flicked. One minute I was standing by the cedar tree, perfectly dry, and the next I was soaking wet and racing up the garden with David.

'I'd say that's it for today, wouldn't you?' he said, sort of laughing and wiping the rainwater from his face. 'Come inside and dry off; we can have a bite to eat and if it still hasn't stopped raining I'll take you home.'

We were sitting at the long kitchen table eating sandwiches when Sophie came into the room carrying the baby. For once it wasn't actually crying and I peered over at the wriggling little one.

'What's her name?' I asked.

Sophie just shrugged her shoulders. 'We can't decide, can we?'

David shook his head. 'We were hoping Alice would help us choose.'

When he said her name, I felt awkward and for a second I wanted to go home, but Sophie had another idea about what we could do while it was raining.

'Come on,' David said and we climbed up the hidden wooden spiral staircase that Alice had told me all about and I saw that the room at the top of the stairs must be Alice's bedroom. I'm not some kind of clever detective or anything like that, but there was, like, a massive pink and silver ALICE sign on the door. We climbed up another narrow flight of stairs to the attic room, but it wasn't creepy and full of cobwebs. In fact, by the time we'd got to it, the rain had stopped as quickly as it started, so the room was actually really bright and sunny. It was kind of huge and it had these sort of high-up windows that I could just about see out of. They looked down over the gardens so you had a kind of bird's eye view of everywhere.

I could see the walled garden where the roses are and the door that goes down to the beach. I looked over to the cedar tree and past the fields out to sea where a lone white sailing boat was moving fast along the shore. I looked right down the beach and towards the harbour wall, and I could just about see the cottage, the marshes and Porlock Hill where I had discovered George, his amazing collection of cars and the glass house that kind of looked like it was from another planet.

'Right, Zack,' David said, looking around at the piles of boxes and unwanted bits of furniture. 'Over there are some of Alice's old baby clothes and Sophie wants us to bring them downstairs. She said to look for the boxes marked nought to one years and I'll go dig out some of my old books for you; you might like them.'

OK, so it wasn't the best job that I'd ever been given and I would've much preferred to be outside rather than searching through boxes of baby stuff. I lifted up one box, then another and another. It took me ages to find the right one and, as I pulled it down from the pile, it slipped out of my hand and skidded right across the floor to the far corner of the attic. I wandered over and bent down to pick it up, but as I did something caught my eye. A door. A slightly open door.

I craned my neck to look and, to my surprise, I saw there was actually another little room. Without thinking, I slowly pushed open the door and stepped inside. I looked around me. Hanging from the ceiling were little planes and, as I reached out to one of them, I took a deep breath. A Tiger Moth. Its wings had been painted very carefully and every single detail was perfect. No smudges, no dripped paint, no mistakes. They hung all around me like Christmas tree decorations and I realised that I could name them all. We could have named them all.

I walked over to the little table and looked down at the model that was sitting half finished. I stared down at the wings, one grey, one red, and I heard his voice. '*Zack, just hold the brush like this,*' he'd say. '*Take it easy, you only need a little bit of paint, Zack,*' he'd tell me, but I wasn't really very good at it. I had dripped the paint everywhere. I got the wrong colours on the wings and finally I'd just given up. In the end I just liked to watch Dad. I didn't mind just watching or passing him the paints or cleaning the brushes. I was happy just doing that.

'In the winter, during those endlessly wet days we have here on Exmoor, me, my brother and our friends used to practically live up here. Your mum and my sister used to have a doll's house up here that they painted blue.'

I looked around at the attic and immediately imagined a group of friends hiding out as the rain and thunder rattled the windows. But then I remembered the two photographs I'd seen. There were five, weren't there? That's what George had said too: 'the Famous Five'. My mum, David, his brother and sister made four, but who was the fifth? Who was the boy with the dimples and curly hair in the photos?

'Kirran was the kindest of all of us, my brother the bravest and your mum was . . .'

'The loudest?' I said and laughed.

David nodded. 'Something like that.'

I reached out and touched another perfectly painted plane.

'My brother did that one. I remember it like yesterday. At first he used to make me watch him paint the models because I was just rubbish at it. I was completely hopeless,' he said, sort of laughing, and it made me smile again and then the two of us seemed to stop smiling at the exact same time.

We stood like that for ages, together, silently, but it didn't feel very quiet.

'I'm not very good at that either,' I said, looking up at the wings of a beautifully painted plane.

'Tom was better than me at most things: cleverer, faster, braver. He did everything fearlessly. I used to just follow him around, trying to copy everything he did. When he painted this one,' David said, touching the Tiger Moth with his fore-finger and smiling, 'he hung it on that piece of string, pointed at his chest and said: "Me tiger, you moth."'

We left the little room and headed back downstairs. As we reached the spiral staircase, I said, 'Is he still, you know, better at most things?'

He suddenly stopped, but he didn't turn round; instead he took a deep breath and softly said, 'He would have been, Zack, but he died a long time ago. When I was about your age.'

'What happened to him?' I blurted out without thinking and it was ages before he answered me. At first I thought he was going to be cross or something; my mum would have gone mental if she'd heard me. She's always telling me off for asking things I shouldn't. I stared at his back and gripped the box of baby clothes for what felt like an eternity, and when he spoke again it was in a weird voice; it was kind of serious, but like he was really far away or something.

'He drowned. He drowned at Culver Cove.'

I held my breath. Was that what Mum had been about to tell me last night?

David didn't turn round again, but if he'd seen my face at that moment I bet he would have guessed. And, as I followed him back through the house, I felt my heart beat quickly and I swear that he could hear it.

In that moment I knew that David, Mum, Sophie, no one could ever know what nearly happened to Alice. No one could know that she'd followed me like a little moth and nearly drowned as well.

It had to always be our secret and Alice had to get better.

31

Alice

I am Alice Isabella Richardson and today I opened my eyes to see my mother asleep in the chair beside my bed, and on the table the photograph of my other mother was propped up against a pile of books.

Last night I dreamt of her again. I dreamt of my other mother. It was a dream that seemed to change and yet it was just the same. She was trying to find me; she was always trying to reach me. She was on a plane surrounded by fog. She ran to the station, but the train left without her. She was on a big red bus that broke down. She was in a car and it ran out of petrol. She was on a bicycle with a flat tyre. She was running up the beach, but she wasn't getting any closer. She was swimming round the headland and kept getting dragged out to sea. She was at the gates to Culver Manor, but they were locked, and when I opened my eyes again I think I knew why. She didn't look after me because she couldn't and the churning, burning feeling started to melt away.

It was as though the bad feeling that had been pressing down on me suddenly lifted and I felt like me again. I felt like Alice once more.

It was like the time me and Florence had been dressing up in Mum's clothes and I'd broken her special necklace. I had tried to tug it over my head and the chain suddenly snapped. Florence and I had watched in horror as the creamy white pearls clattered on to the wooden floor and rolled under the bed. For some reason I didn't want to tell Mum. I didn't want to upset her. The necklace had been her mother's and her grandmother's so, instead of telling her, me and Florence had collected up all the pearls and hidden them in a sock at the back of my wardrobe.

At first Mum hadn't noticed. Even when Florence and her family left to go back to Scotland she still hadn't realised that the necklace was missing, but when she did it was horrible. She raced round the house, turning out drawers; she pulled everything out of her wardrobe and emptied the cupboards in her bathroom. I saw her walk quickly past my bedroom and into my bathroom, muttering all the time, '*I can't have lost it, please let me find it.*'

As every hour went by, I felt myself getting more and more nervous. As each box was emptied out and searched through, I told myself to confess. The more upset I saw my mum getting, the harder it became so, when she asked me if I'd seen it, I lied.

I hardly slept at all that night and when I came down for breakfast I couldn't even eat anything. I saw Mum gazing out of the window and when Dad came in he bent down in front of her and wiped a tear away from her cheek and kissed her. I watched her take two deep breaths and then she turned to me, smiled and said, 'So then, Alice, if you don't fancy croissants, how about I make you some French toast instead?'

Perhaps it was something in her smile or the way her pale grey eyes looked at me so kindly, but when I opened my mouth to answer her the whole story came blurting out of me. By the time I'd finished telling them both what had happened, I was crying so hard I could barely talk. I expected the biggest telling-off ever. I expected to be shouted at and sent to my bedroom. I told myself that I deserved the biggest and worst punishment ever, but Mum just threw her arms round me and cried.

We almost ran up the stairs to my bedroom together and when she saw the sock with all the pearls inside she sort of laughed. And, as she tipped the pearls out on to the bed and counted them all, she laughed, looked at me, smiling again. 'You must have felt horrible. You must have been more upset than me. But you never need to be scared of telling me the truth, Alice. Doesn't it feel much better?' And she was right. As I looked into her happy eyes again, I did feel so much better.

I looked at my mum now. Her eyes were closed; a strand of blonde hair hung down across her face. Her pale hands lay folded on her lap. She wore a white nightdress with a lilac shawl around her shoulders. The sunlight shone across her face so that I could see the little hairs on her pale cheeks.

I looked back to my other mother, held my hand out towards the photograph, traced my fingertip along her face, her long dark hair and I whispered something softly.

I lay back on the pillow; my eyes were tired, my head still ached and I closed my eyes to think some more. I heard the sound of the house martins chirruping at the window where they had come back to nest again. They always came back, I thought, they always found their way back to Culver Manor, and I pulled the covers up to my chin and fell asleep.

32

Zack

Alice is getting better.

'Alice is going to be fine,' David told me as we drank lemonade on the terrace, and I felt happier and more relieved than I've felt my whole entire life, and I kind of stayed feeling like that all day. Which was good because I spent quite a lot of that day in a very small space, tripping over stuff and banging my head.

When David saw what I'd done, when he saw that I hadn't dripped the paint all over the lawn (well, I did, but I just put my foot over that bit), he was really impressed.

'Have you done this sort of thing before, Zack?'

'Yeah,' I said, thinking of the shed me and Dad had built at our old house. I rubbed the thumb that was still a bit sore from where George had got the splinter out and I remembered how Dad had really bashed his own thumb with the hammer. He'd been telling me how I had to be really careful with all the tools, but he'd been looking at me as he banged the nail into the wall. 'Like this,' he said as his hand slipped and the hammer came down hard against his thumb. As he shouted out all the various swear words I'd ever heard, he sort of laughed and said, 'But definitely don't do it like *that*, Zack.'

David sighed and put the lid back on the pale blue paint pot. 'Well, have you enjoyed it?'

I looked up at what we'd made. I thought about how many more little splinters I'd got in my fingers and how many times I'd banged my head, and I looked at him, grinned and said, 'It was cool.'

We stood like that for ages, just kind of looking, and then I realised that we were both just staring down the garden across the sea and out to Wales. I looked at David and then a sad feeling came over me because, now that we'd finished, what else would I do every day when Mum was at work? Would I have to go back to the cottage and sit on my own all day until school started? I looked round at the garden and up to the house. I felt the sun warm the backs of my arms, I took a gulp of Sophie's home-made lemonade, I breathed in the lovely flowery smell, I listened to the sound of waves on the beach below and I knew I wanted to stay here forever.

And, as if he could read my mind, David smiled and said, 'Would you like to earn a bit of pocket money, Zack?'

So, while I waited for Alice to be well enough to come down from her bedroom, I did all sorts of jobs in the garden. I did this thing where you take the dead flowers off the plants, I stacked the logs in neat piles, I brought in all the different vegetables and that's when I saw Mum's favourite food.

'Asparagus,' David said when he saw me looking. I loved the way they tasted, but I'd never seen them grow up out of the ground like funny green pencils. I realised that tomatoes could actually be yellow as well as red, but I preferred the way the really little ones tasted and David had to tell me to stop gobbling them all up. I spent ages in the herb garden getting rid of weeds and things, but I hated doing that. That was, like, the worst job ever, but the best thing was the lawn-mower. It was the sort that you sit on, like a kind of motor-bike with a grass cutter attached to it. It was probably the coolest thing and I was even allowed to have a little go all by myself, and I worked out how to go backwards round one of the apple trees, although David wasn't really laughing when I did it a bit too fast and kind of drove over a special kind of plant.

'Hmm,' he said, frowning. 'Er, Jenson Button, a little less speed, if you don't mind.'

But he was sort of smiling at the same time and that's when I realised that David isn't like other grown-ups. He doesn't say things like: 'Don't do that, don't do this, do it my way, stop doing that.' He sort of likes telling jokes, and when I asked him what Somerset Vale was like he locked the door of the shed and said, 'If it was good enough for me, it'll be good enough for you.'

I thought I was going to have to go home, but Sophie said I could stay for dinner and Mum came too. She chatted for ages with David. They told me how, when they were younger, they had camped out in the walled garden one night, but David laughed and said, 'Yeah, but I got a bit scared and went back in the house.'

Mum seemed to be very interested in the screaming baby that still didn't have a name.

'I thought it would be like it was with Alice,' I heard Sophie say, 'but David and I can't agree. I like the name Alexia, but David prefers Emma. We're going to have to decide soon though.'

Then my mum said something that I didn't know. 'Zack didn't have a name for the first three weeks of his life, and then Jonathan read this amazing book about the famous mountain climber, Edward Ellroy. The first time he climbed Everest he broke his leg on the way down. Normally he would have just died, but a man who was climbing up the mountain saved his life. That man gave up his oxygen and his own climb to the summit just to save Ellroy's life. He was called Novak Zachariah.'

I looked across the table at Mum and she smiled.

'But,' I said, sort of confused and upset, 'I thought I was named after the famous climber.'

David took a big gulp of his beer and grinned at me. 'Nah, Zack, it's better than that. You were named after a truly great man. The best sort of man. The bravest kind. A man who thinks of others first.'

I thought of my dad. He was the bravest, wasn't he?

When we'd got home and Mum came to say goodnight, I asked her the question I'd wanted to ask since she told the story.

'Mum, would Dad have done that? Would Dad have saved the man on the mountain?'

She smiled, kissed my forehead and said, 'Every time, Zack. Every time.'

I was going to ask her about what happened to David's brother. I was going to ask about the group of friends, but I didn't want to make her sad.

I lay awake for ages and thought that when I was at Culver Manor all the worries stopped being worries. It wasn't the super-scary place I'd imagined, Alice's mum and dad were not the strict ogre 'lock-you-up-in-the-attic' type parents and Porlock Weir wasn't the dull and boring place I'd once thought it was going to be either. But when I did fall asleep I had this stupid sort of nightmare where I was at my new school, but I was naked and everyone was standing around me, laughing.

In the morning I couldn't wait to get up to Culver Manor and leave all the horrid feeling behind. I think I practically ran the whole way there and when I got there Sophie had the best news ever.

33

Alice

Today I sat up in bed for the first time. I still can't really hear out of one ear, but I have two ears so that's not so bad. I feel really hungry; when I move, I'm not in any pain and the light no longer hurts my eyes. I woke to the sound of crying and when I turned to look I saw the photograph of my other mother, and Mum was sitting in a chair next to the bed. I looked at her and smiled.

'That is a lovely sight to see, Alice.'

Dad placed a delicious tray of food on my bed and, as I gobbled the sandwiches and slurped up the milkshake, they told me everything that had happened while I'd been ill, but, one thing was clear, no one but Zack and I knew that I had tried to swim round the headland or that Zack had saved my life. I decided there and then that it would always be our secret.

*   *   *

That evening I sat up in bed and read for a little while, drew inside my notebook, and it must have been really late when Mum came back to sit with me. At first I didn't see her and then I heard a gurgling sound and my little sister let us know she was hungry. I watched her little pink face get redder and redder. I saw her tiny hands clench into tiny fists, but her eyes stayed tightly shut. I watched Mum as she started to feed her. The crying stopped immediately, but her eyes stayed closed. For some reason I wanted to touch the little pink thing which wriggled about, but when I held my hand out something strange happened. As my hand reached hers, she stopped sucking. As my finger hovered above her hands, she stopped drinking, turned towards me and opened her eyes. I looked up at Mum and smiled.

Dad slowly crept into the room and sat down on my bed.

'She's beautiful, isn't she?' Dad said and I nodded.

'She doesn't have a name yet,' Mum said, looking up at me, smiling hopefully. I sat up and wriggled closer to Dad. I took his arm, pulled it round my waist and I felt him kiss the top of my head. I let my feet dangle down from the bed so that my toes were touching the top of Mum's feet, so that I could feel her soft skin beneath mine. I leaned in closer to my dad and stroked the hairs on his freckly arms. All the questions stopped being questions. All the bad feeling that was churning in my stomach was gone. It was just like it used to be, but something made it better.

I peered over the blanket at my little sister. She *was* beautiful, she really was. With her tiny hand, she reached up, gripped my finger and stared right at me. She seemed to stare at me as though she would never stop. Her little hand seemed to hold on so tightly I thought she would never let go. As she began to drink again, her eyes stayed fixed on mine, and when I tried to pull my finger free she gripped it even tighter. She was so small. Smaller than small. Tinier than tiny. I stared back at her eyes, smiled and after six months of silence I looked up at Dad and Mum and softly said: 'Rebecca.'

Mum and Dad looked at each other quickly and then they both smiled.

'Rebecca Richardson,' Mum said.

'Rebecca,' Dad sort of whispered. 'It's perfect.'

Now my little sister has a name.

It was Tuesday August 27th when I sat up in bed and felt like me again. My eyes sort of pinged open. I jumped out of bed, pulled back the curtains and when I looked down the garden to the cedar tree I saw something which made my heart sing.

I didn't walk down the hallway, I ran. I didn't run down the stairs, I jumped two steps at a time, and I didn't stop until I felt the wet grass under my bare feet and I was standing right under the cedar tree, looking up at it.

'It's amazing!' I shouted. 'It's perfect!' I cried. 'It's the best tree house in the whole world!'

And just then Zack stuck his head out from the little window and said, 'That's exactly what I said.'

He let down a little rope ladder and I climbed all the way up. The first room was sort of square and it had a kind of rectangular window that looked down across the fields and out to sea. It was like a perfect little wooden house, and there was even enough room for two beanbags and a table. The walls were painted a sort of pale blue, like the colour of the stones on the beach. On one wall there was a huge map so that you could see the whole of the vale and out to sea to the little island where no one lives.

'It's cool, isn't it?' Zack said, showing me the three little steps which led up to another smaller room that also had a kind of window. 'It's a two-tier tree house and I helped make it.'

And the best thing about it was this. At one end of the tree house was a hole that you could fit through and slide down to the ground on a sort of fireman's pole which is exactly what I did. In fact, I did it three more times until I heard a familiar, horrid, whiny voice, and when I looked out of the window I saw the toady face that it belonged to. Casper. I'd forgotten all about him and Florence coming to stay, and as I looked up the lawn to the terrace I saw Aunt Aggy and Florence walking across the terrace towards Mum.

'Let me up!' Casper demanded, folding his arms across his chest and tapping his foot.

'Who is that?' Zack asked, peering down the hole.

'It's Casper, my cousin,' I said, pulling a face.

'Let me up now!' he yelled, his pasty face getting redder.

'Quick,' said Zack and he pulled the rope ladder back up into the tree house just in time to see a red-faced Casper glare up at us.

'I want to come up!' he shouted. 'Let me up now!' But Zack and I just laughed, and when he tried to climb up the fireman's pole the two of us laughed so loudly that I think the whole of Porlock Weir must have heard us. 'I'm telling! I'm telling Mummy!' he cried.

Zack, who was trying to stop laughing, just shouted back, 'NO ONE likes a telltale, Casper!'

We stayed up there until Mum shouted at me to come inside and get dressed, but before I slid down the pole Zack said, 'Will you tell? I mean, seeing as you're all better and everything?' He looked scared, really worried, and I shook my head and crossed my heart.

I raced back inside the house. I heard Rebecca before I saw her. Mum looked really tired again, poor Mum; it's actually hard work looking after something so tiny. I followed her upstairs to the nursery. I stood at the door and watched her carefully lift Rebecca out of my old cot and when she turned to me she took my hand in hers. We walked slowly down the hall together until we reached the big windows that look out on to the garden. She sat down in the middle window and I sat next to her. Then she showed me how to hold my little sister. I held my arms out and delicately cradled Rebecca so that her head was resting on my arm and she was safe and snug.

Have you ever held a baby? Have you held one close to your heart? It made me feel like a giant. It made me feel like

I was holding on to something that could break. At first I was scared and I looked up at Mum worriedly.

'Don't worry,' she whispered. 'You'll be fine.'

When Rebecca opened her eyes, she stared right at me again and I smiled. Then she opened her mouth and, I don't know why, but I thought she might just say hello, so I did.

'Hello,' I said softly. 'Hello, Rebecca. I'm Alice. I'm your big sister.'

I looked down at the tiny warm bundle. I felt her wriggle and squirm about, and I kind of liked it. It was a bit like a doll that I used to take everywhere except this was better; this little doll actually moved around and looked at me. This Rebecca really belonged to me.

Mum handed me a tiny bottle of milk and, without thinking or knowing, without even being told how, I lifted it to her dainty pink mouth and I fed her. She sucked and sucked, and it made me giggle a bit and feel special and grown-up.

'Alice,' Mum said softly. 'When you became our daughter, when I held you for the first time, I was scared. I was scared, but I was the happiest I had ever been in my whole life. It makes me very happy to see you hold your sister. I love you both very much.'

I looked up from Rebecca to Mum's pale face and saw the tears roll down her cheeks and land on her lilac shawl like little silver droplets of rain.

'She would have loved you so much,' she said and she leaned over to me and kissed my forehead. 'She would have loved you if she could have.'

For some reason it made me think of Otter. It made me think of Zack's gorgeous brown dog. I remembered the dream I had had and I understood. I thought about the photograph of my other mother and then I said, 'Where is she now?'

Mum didn't say anything for a while, but I could see her concentrating hard as though she was trying to put the words together, but kept getting mixed up. 'We don't know a lot about her. We know she was very young when she had you, and that she didn't have a family to help her, and that she was from London.'

As I listened to her, it was as though it didn't matter. As she told me a little tiny bit about the mother who had given me away, I found that I didn't care in the way I thought I would. My other mother gave me away for a reason: so I could find my real mother who was sitting right in front of me.

I looked up at Mum's tear-stained face and then down at my beautiful, most perfect little sister. 'Mum, you are, like, totally crying on Rebecca now, look,' I said, wiping one of Mum's tears from Rebecca's cheek, and Mum smiled at me again. I sniffed the air and wrinkled my nose. 'Was that you, Mum, or Rebecca?' And we both laughed.

'I'm so proud of you, Alice,' Mum said, kissing the tip of my nose, and then she pulled me close towards her. I turned round and sat with my back against her, so that she had her arms round me and I had mine round my beautiful baby sister. We sat like that for ages and when Rebecca finished her milk she closed her eyes again and fell asleep holding on to my little finger.

I didn't say anything for a while, but then the rain began. It started with tiny droplets that rattled on the windowpane and very soon the sky seemed to have turned almost black and there was a waterfall of water. Mum reached up with one hand and pulled the curtain round us so that we were hidden on the window seat, so that it was just the three of us.

'Mum, how come you and Dad said the footpath to the cove was covered in rocks and things? How come we never went down there because I think it's amazing?'

She didn't say anything for ages and, as I looked down at Rebecca, she told me a story that I had never heard before. I listened with the widest eyes. I heard every letter of every word, and in the end I knew the real reason why the beach had been closed off and it all made perfect sense. And I knew that Zack and I must keep our secret for ever and ever.

The next day Rebecca stayed at home with my aunt and uncle, but Dad said, 'There's only one thing to do on a hot day like this,' and Mum, Casper, Florence and me followed him through the rose garden where the red rose bush had now been cut back to reveal the overgrown door which I had found.

'Wow!' Florence said when she saw the door. 'That is, like, so cool,' and, as we walked down the footpath, I told her all about the story I had heard from Mum. When we got to the waterfall, she turned to me and, tying her long hair in a sort of messy bun, she said, 'It's all beginning to make sense now, isn't it?' I nodded. I wanted to tell Zack all about it too, but Mum had said I shouldn't talk about it too much in case it made Dad feel sad.

When we got to the beach, Zack was there with his body-board and for the first time ever I realised that Casper wasn't being annoying.

'Is it true?' Florence asked as we looked for shells together. 'Is it true you named your sister?'

I looked over at Zack and smiled. 'Yes, it's true.' And just then I spotted the perfect pink shell. It made me think of Rebecca's little pink mouth and I picked it off the sand. 'For Rebecca,' I said, holding up the shell for Florence to see.

'It's perfect,' she said, looping her arm into mine and the two of us lay in the sun until we got so hot that there was only one thing to do: run as fast as we could into the sea and dive right under.

That night it was like I was the mum or something because I got to give Rebecca a bath. Well, Mum was in the bathroom too, but I got to fill the little bath up, make sure the water wasn't too hot and I used the little sponge to wash her softest-ever skin. Mum wrapped Rebecca in a big white fluffy towel and we carried her back to the nursery. As Mum dried her off, I placed the pink shell on the chest by her music box.

'For luck,' I said.

Mum reached out and stroked my face. 'She doesn't need luck. She has you.'

Later, as I climbed into bed, I picked up the photograph of my other mother and took a closer look. The thing that was so familiar wasn't the street she stood on or the shop she was standing in front of; it was her eyes. I'd seen them before. I'd seen them every time I looked in the mirror. We did look alike. We had the exact same eyes and smile.

I opened the drawer and placed the photograph inside. I knew I'd look at it again, but there wasn't really enough room on my bedside table for two photographs, all my books *and* shells from the beach. So, gently, I put the photo away and softly closed the drawer.

That night, as I was falling asleep, I heard the owls in the woods, the waves as they crashed on to the beach and I thought of Rebecca again. Would she grow up to be as tall as Dad? Would she have hair like Mum? Or would she love swimming in the sea just like me? And in the morning I couldn't wait to see her.

34

Zack

Yesterday Alice saw the world's greatest tree house.

I thought I was going to have to lock her annoying cousin Casper in the shed at the back of the vegetable garden. At first I really thought I might have to do something drastic, and when he started whining about nothing much I waited till no one was looking and gave him a really good dead arm instead. He turned round and glared at me, and for a milli-second I was kind of worried that he would scream the place down. But after that he kind of stopped being a complete brat and followed me around all day which was a little less annoying.

Alice's other cousin Florence is sort of OK; she's really pretty and everything, but she's not as cool as Alice and she's a bit like: 'I live in a castle', 'I have three ponies', 'I'm so great'. But when we all went down to Culver again she spent the whole time with Alice and every time I looked over Alice was laughing or doing one of her silly animal walks.

The next day Mum drove me up the hill to visit George, and when we got there the two of them hugged for ages, and when I looked at George he wiped a tear away from his cheek.

'He's going to lend us one of his collection for the day,' Mum said and I immediately thought about the Ferrari again. But it *so* wasn't a Ferrari. It was a sort of camper van thing and as I waited for Mum to finish her cup of tea I wandered into the barn and over to the plane once more, but I didn't touch it.

'Fancy going up in her one day?'

I turned round quickly and shook my head at George.

'Well, if you ever change your mind,' he said and walked away. Part of me wanted to cry out after him, but part of me knew that I couldn't.

It took over an hour to drive the little van down the coast road and when I started to feel a bit carsick I kind of wished I hadn't eaten five pancakes for breakfast. Mum parked the little van near the sand dunes and, as I looked down the vast windy beach, I couldn't get in my wetsuit quick enough. The waves were almost perfect. Even Mum put her wetsuit on and the two of us bodyboarded until my arms ached and my eyes stung, but I didn't care.

That night the two of us lit a campfire and cooked a sort of supper and a pudding of toasted marshmallows that tasted so delicious I had to fight to have the last one. We lay back on our little beds with tired bodies and stuffed-to-bursting tummies, and I asked her the question I'd been wanting to ask since the time I was in the attic with David.

'Mum, what were you going to tell me that night? What happened on the beach when you were younger?'

It was ages before Mum answered. She turned on her back so that I could just see the outline of her face and, for the first time ever, she found a way to speak softly, slowly in a voice that was like she was almost whispering.

'It was always just the five of us. Five of us together. No one else was allowed to join in and no one tried to leave. Just the five of us. Tom, David, Aggy, me and Kirran. Kirran Moore. The kindest, sweetest boy. The gentlest, most patient boy. The best of all of us.

'Tom was the bravest one, that's for sure. Nothing ever seemed to frighten him. A spider the size of a saucer, a jelly-fish the size of a football, a rat the size of a small cat. Before it happened, we all practically lived up at Culver. The winters were spent hiding out in the attic and every dry summer's day we went down to the cove. We were always careful and never broken the golden rule: don't try and swim round the headland.

'Every day of the summer holidays I would meet Kirran at the little stone bridge near our cottage and the two of us would race up to the manor with his little dog Spice. He loved that dog. Not that Spice liked anyone but Kirran though. We'd run up to Culver, through the gates and down to the secret door. Aggy always needed help jumping over the ledge and Kirran was a bit scared too, but Tom wasn't scared of anything and would leap over it with his eyes shut, and everything that Tom did David did too.

'That day we got to the beach later than normal. The tide was already in and then an argument began. Tom and Kirran were playing tennis or something and then started bickering about a point. At first it was just a jokey fight, but then it got louder and more serious until I looked up and saw Tom throw the tennis ball into the water. He threw it really hard and it went far out to sea. Wherever a tennis ball went, Spice was sure to follow. I remember seeing Spice practically fly off the rocks after the yellow ball and splash loudly into the water. Kirran shouted after him to come back, but the poor dog was determined to get his ball back.

'David started yelling at Tom for being stupid, saying that Spice wouldn't be able to reach the ball; he was so cross with him. We all watched Spice swim right out into the cove. Kirran was so worried about him . . .' Mum paused and wiped a tear from her face. 'Then Kirran ran into the water too and desperately started to swim towards Spice. None of us knew what to do. Kirran wasn't a strong swimmer, but he wouldn't just leave Spice out there.

'I was screaming at the boys to do something, and Aggy was doing the same. Tom was the only one of us who stood a chance of reaching Kirran and we all knew that, so he ran into the water after him. He swam out towards the head-land, but it was too late . . . Spice and Kirran were pulled under, we saw their heads bob below the water from the beach, but even then Tom didn't give up; he just kept going. And then . . . then the current got him too. He was pulled under. Gone. Spice, Kirran and Tom, all just gone. There one moment, not the next. It was terrible. We went to the beach that day as five friends and we came back as three.

'After that, the family closed the beach off. Culver Manor got gloomier and gloomier. David's mum and dad became sadder and sadder until one day they shut the house up and never came back. I snuck in through the gates one day. I think it was the day before I left for university. I couldn't believe how overgrown it was. How sad it looked. That's when I took the photograph I showed you.'

Mum paused, but kept staring at the sky.

I looked at her and even in the darkness I could see the tears glistening in her eyes. I lay there silently and thought of Alice. Did she know this story too? Is that why she was so afraid of being discovered?

So that night, the day after I turned thirteen, Mum and I fell asleep in the camper van to the sound of crickets and crashing waves, and a million thoughts swam around my head.

When we got home, I ran upstairs to put my stuff away and I spotted my new school uniform hanging up. I'd forgotten all about starting school on Monday and suddenly all the

218

good feelings I had went away. I just felt totally sick instead. I sat down on the bed and wanted to stop the day from going any further. If my dad was still alive, I wouldn't have to be doing all this.

Mum said I had to be brave. She always says I'm really like him, but most of the time I think I can't be anything like him because I get really frightened of stuff all the time. And now I'll never get to fly across the Channel just like he did because he isn't here to show me, is he? And I've decided that being super brave, being really brave like my dad was or like the man I was named after, is not something that you can learn. I think it's something that you either are or aren't and, as I was too scared to go up in an aeroplane again, I must be the least brave boy on the whole planet.

I looked down at the name tag that Mum had sewn into my new school jumper and felt myself get upset. I didn't deserve to be named after someone so amazing after all.

I went downstairs and when Mum saw my miserable face she said we should go for a walk, but instead of walking along the beach towards the headland we turned right along the bay. There was a little footpath that went all the way alongside it and, as we crossed a little stone bridge, I saw David and Alice just ahead.

'Hey, Zack!' she shouted and the two of us ran ahead along the marshes, but I didn't really feel like saying much so I let Alice chatter on about her sister. Rebecca this, Rebecca that, on and on she went, and when she offered me one of her Haribos I still felt sort of too sick.

I just looked down at the ground and shook my head.

'Are *you* going to stop talking now?' she asked me with a grin.

For some reason it made me stop and I just stared back at her angrily.

'Haribos?' she said, holding out the packet, and I don't know why, but I just snatched the whole bag off her, threw it as far as I could.

'I already said I don't want any of your stupid sweets, ALICE! FOR GOD'S SAKE!' I shouted at her.

I thought she'd run away or something, but she didn't. So I decided that I didn't actually want to be with anyone at all and I walked away from her, off the path and out of sight. Actually, I almost slipped out of sight because the marshes were really muddy. I could hear Alice shouting my name and when I turned back I could see the bay curving back towards the village, and I could just make out the back of our cottage and my bedroom window.

I ran up the steps of a little wooden bridge, but as I reached the other side my foot sort of slipped and I went flying forward. I went flying, flying, landing kind of on my knees, and when I pulled myself up I saw it. At first I had no clue what I was looking at because it just looked like a sort of gravestone. I must have been staring at it for ages when I heard Alice catch up with me, and when she saw what I was staring at she looked a bit worried.

I turned back to the stone and read the sign that was next to it.

On October 29th 1942 US Air Force Liberator Bomber lost in fog clipped the hill at Bossington and crashed on these marshes killing seven out of the eight crew members.

'Dad says they were real war heroes,' Alice whispered.

I read the names.

I read the names again and that was when I felt something. I read the names out loud and I heard my dad shouting for me. His little yellow plane flashed in front of my eyes and I felt like I was falling. I saw the tiny pots of paint and the model that we had tried to make together. I saw Dad laughing when he saw I'd stuck the wing of an F14 on to a Harrier. I saw Dad's plane as it hit the ground that day. I saw him carving the roast chicken and having a sneaky slice before we all sat down. I saw the yellow and orange flames. I saw him wink at me when he pretended he'd forgotten Mum's birthday, but he'd actually hidden the beautiful necklace inside her box of cereal. I saw him grab my skateboard and show me how not to fall off. I saw the ambulance arriving at the airfield and the firemen racing towards the flames. I saw Dad as he ate one of Mum's terrible mince pies and pretended that it was nice. I saw his face upside down as we both did backflips off the boat. I saw his plane explode as the flames reached the fuel tank. I felt his huge hands round my waist as he lifted me up to put the little robin on top of the Christmas tree. The prickle of his face against mine. The smell of the outdoors on his skin. His widest smile and the little chip on his front tooth. The sound of his deep voice as he read me bedtime stories which he always used to change. He'd always change the names so that I was in the story. 'This is our story,' he'd tell me, 'and we can make it into anything we want.'

I looked up at the sign once again. *Sole survivor.* One of them had made it. I suddenly dropped down to my knees. I felt the cool marsh mud on my skin and, with a heaving swell of pain that pressed down on my chest, I cried. I cried for the first time and I didn't ever think I would stop.

35

Alice

Zack looked up at me and I watched the tears roll down his cheeks. I saw his body shake.

'I'll never be like Dad,' he sobbed.

I saw his hands clench at the muddy ground and I knew what I had to do. I turned round and ran back to Dad and Jane. They had stopped on the far side of the little wooden bridge and were chatting. I could see Dad was laughing at something Jane had just said, and I knew that by the time I had finished he would not be smiling or laughing at all. I had to do it, I told myself. I had to tell my dad the amazing thing that Zack had done, even if it meant telling him I had almost drowned like his brother, Kirran and Spice. I had to tell the truth even if it meant telling Mum and Dad that the reason I had got so poorly wasn't just because

I'd been for a swim, but because I'd tried to swim round the headland.

I just knew I had to tell the truth, but as I reached them I started to slow down. What would he say? What would he do? I walked slowly across the bridge and waited. I opened my mouth to speak, but the words got stuck. I felt my heart beat faster and faster, and in the end I stayed sort of stuck on the middle of the bridge, stuck halfway between speaking and not speaking.

I turned my head back in the direction of Zack and I thought of him kneeling in the mud. I thought of him crying like I'd never seen anyone cry, so I turned back to Dad and told him as quickly and simply as I could.

Dad stared. Jane stared and for a moment I was terrified.

'You did what?' Dad said, walking towards me. 'You did what?' he said, looking puzzled.

'I didn't mean to. I hadn't meant to. Please don't be mad,' I begged.

'You tried to swim round the headland?' he said, kneeling in front of me, and then I whispered into his ear. I told my dad the truth. I told him mine and Zack's secret and he looked more shocked than he ever had. I looked up at Jane and I told her too.

'He did what?' I watched her and Dad suddenly look at each other and shake their heads.

We all sort of ran across the marshes together and, when we finally got to Zack, Jane was running so fast she sort of skidded the last bit and got covered in marsh mud. Zack was exactly where I had left him. His face was red and swollen, and his whole body kind of jerked back and forth as the last of his tears left his body. Jane walked over and knelt down beside him.

'I'm not brave, M . . . M . . . Mum,' he sobbed. 'I'm scared. I'll never be as brave as D . . . Dad,' he cried and she helped him to his feet. He seemed to sort of crumple into her arms and his whole body seemed to shrink in towards her so that Zack looked like a tiny little child, and it made me feel so sad I tugged on Dad's sleeve and looked up at him as if to say, 'Do something, make it better.'

'Zack,' my dad said slowly. 'Zack Ethan Drake,' he said, taking my hand and walking over to them.

Zack's red and tear-stained face turned to us and when I looked at my dad I could see that there was a tear running down his cheek too. 'Zack Ethan Drake,' he said softly. 'Did you save my daughter's life?'

Zack's eyes darted to mine with a look of fear and almost anger, but I smiled back and willed him to tell the truth. He looked up at my dad and slowly nodded.

'Well, Zack, I'd say that you are just about the bravest person I have ever met.'

And he was.

36

Zack

I think Alice is probably my best friend, but I haven't decided yet. She keeps telling me that I'm *her* best friend so it might be true.

The night before my first day at school I lay awake for ages. *I'll probably get beaten up. I'll probably trip over in front of everyone or do something stupid.* In the end I got out of bed and went downstairs, but Mum was still up. She was sitting at the table with a towel wrapped round her head and a kind of magazine with lots of pictures of women with strange-looking hair. *Great,* I thought, *Mum's hair will be, like, pink or something and she'll wear one of those crazy dresses she always wears.*

I went back upstairs and knelt down beside the bed. I scrabbled around under it until my hands reached the corner of the photograph frame that I'd kicked under the bed when I was really cross. I grabbed at it with my hand and when I pulled it out I kind of smiled. Dad. *Dad, why did you let Mum wear such stupid clothes?* It made me laugh a bit and I put the photograph frame on the table by my bed and climbed in. This time I fell asleep straight away and I dreamt of mountains that were sort of purple and a beach with silver sand.

And in the morning I got the biggest shock. Firstly my new school blazer actually has two inside pockets and Mum did not look like Mum. Her hair wasn't pink or red or orange or white-blonde. It wasn't sticking up in every direction or had a million flowery hairclips in it. It was black, like mine, and it was combed so it looked really normal. I stared at her for ages. She wasn't wearing her board shorts, a flowery dress or those sparkly tops she sometimes does. She had on a plain, bog-standard, very dull, but so not embarrassing pair of navy trousers and a navy jacket too.

For the first time my mum actually looked like a grown-up.

'Well?' she said, looking more nervous than me.

'You look really nice,' I said.

The next thing that happened was a mixture of massively scary and kind of OK. When I got to school, I felt so sick that I really thought I was going to throw up. I had to go to the Headmaster's office and meet the person who was going to be my 'mentor'.

'At Somerset Vale,' he said, peering over his desk at me, 'we always assign a new pupil to an older pupil so one of the Year Eleven boys will be your mentor.'

I had to wait at the reception for what felt like forever. I watched all the other new pupils shuffle into school and that's when I saw that everyone looked like me. Everyone looked scared. I watched a boy who was going to be in my year as he was introduced to a scary-looking mentor, but as soon as the Head turned away the mentor kind of shoved the boy in the back and my heart sank. I think I was just staring at my shoes when I heard a really deep voice say my name.

I guess I expected to see a big man or something, but it was a boy.

'Come on then,' he said.

I slowly stood up and followed him down the corridor. I waited for the punch or the kick or something, and then he stopped by a drinks fountain and turned to look at me.

'Did you really swim round the headland to Culver then?' he said. I stared back at him and tried to think what the right answer would be. I opened my mouth to speak, but the words didn't come and he laughed. 'I'd be well scared, I reckon. I wouldn't have the guts to do that.' And when he saw my confused-looking face he put his arm round my shoulder and said, 'My nan knows everything, mate. She's Pippa, from the post office? I swear she's got some kind of special hearing and she has eyes in the back of her head.'

I didn't get punched. I didn't get kicked and nothing bad happened at all, although my mum waved at me once and I had to ignore her.

It made me think of what George had said to me. 'Nothing is ever as bad as it seems.' And he was right.

37

Alice

Today is September 7th and it is my dad's birthday. Yesterday it rained all day so he went fishing with Zack. They packed the car up with all sorts of fishing rods and a picnic that Mum had made, and I waved them off on the driveway.

'Bring a salmon home for supper!' Mum shouted and we went inside to make him his birthday cake while Becky Boo slept in a little basket on the kitchen table. And later that day, as I was feeding my sister, my mum took a telephone call that went on for ages. I heard her say, 'Oh yes, Jane, what a great idea and why don't they all stay here?' I asked her about it at bedtime, but she just smiled and said, 'Something fun. You'll enjoy it.'

After Dad opened his presents, he went outside to the terrace. 'I've got something I need to do,' he said, taking a toolbox with him, and shortly after that I heard voices outside that I didn't recognise. I raced across the hallway to the spiral staircase and peered out of the little window on to the driveway. There was Zack, his mum, a taller woman, two girls and a dog. It had to be Otter!

The girl with the red hair was the loudest and she was marching up to the front door as though she lived here. And, as though she could sense me looking down, she looked up at the window and waved. I'd never seen anyone with an eyepatch before and I ran back down the stairs to the front door. Standing there with presents in their arms was a woman with curly red hair, a shy-looking girl with short brown hair and the loud one.

'I'm Lexi,' she said loudly. 'Happy birthday!'

The other girl sort of sighed and rolled her eyes. 'Er, Lexi, it's her dad's birthday, remember.' They both kind of laughed and I did too.

'Oh yes, sorry, Mum said. I forgot.' She twirled a strand of curly hair round her finger and laughed nervously. 'I'm always forgetting things.'

Just then the gorgeous brown dog reappeared with Zack and his mum.

'He needed a wee. Alice, this is Otter.' Zack pulled the lead tighter and immediately Otter sat down at his feet. 'Lexi's been teaching him new stuff. Watch.' He unhooked the lead, pointed to the ground and I watched as Otter rolled over on to his back.

Jane laughed. 'Looks like Otter has been at dog-training school, Lexi.'

Then the other girl spoke for the first time. 'Well, it took us about eight goes to get him to do that and he chewed right through my schoolbag afterwards.' Zack laughed and the four of us raced through the garden to the tree house where we stayed until it was time for lunch.

George was the last to arrive and I watched Mum, Dad and Jane hug him tightly and, after we'd eaten, him and Dad sat on my uncle's special bench and chatted until it was getting dark. It was only then that I saw what my dad had needed his toolbox for; it was only when I went back outside to get my jumper that I saw what he had done. Carved into the back of the wooden bench were two names: *Thomas Edward Richardson* and *Kirran Moore*.

We had to go up to the attic to find the really big tent because the one that Lexi and Eddie had brought had a massive hole in it. Dad, George and Zack put it up and in the end George said there was enough room for a football team to camp out in, let alone four children and a dog. The four of us watched the sky nervously. It had to be a clear sky if we were going to do it. We peered out from our tent and I could feel Zack grinning as the biggest moon lit up the garden so brightly it was as though someone had switched the lights on.

'Are you ready then?' Dad said.

'It's going to be chilly,' Jane said nervously, but I thought the air felt as warm as on a summer's day.

Mum said later that she could hear the sound of us all giggling from the house and I think she really must have because Lexi is probably one of the funniest people I have ever met. We used our torches on the footpath, and when Eddie said she couldn't see properly Lexi laughed and said, 'Yeah, try doing it wearing an eyepatch.'

When we got to the little ledge, I saw that it wasn't a little ledge any more. The gap that we used to jump across had been fixed. Instead of a gaping hole there was a wooden step and when I shone my torch down I saw the words that had been carved into it: *One, two, three, jump!* Even the really tricky bits had been made easier and when I looked up at Dad he smiled.

'Well, if we're going to be coming down here all the time, I thought I'd best make it as safe as possible,' he said.

Have you ever swum in the moonlight? Have you ever dived under blackened sea and seen the moon shine down through the silvery waters? It feels like you're swimming through another world. We were careful not to go too far, and my dad was with us the whole time, watching, but we had so much fun splashing around in the sea. We dived again and again under the water, until we were all getting cold, and then the four of us ran back to the shore and wrapped ourselves up in the warmest, softest towels. But before I left the beach I found a stick and drew upon the sand:

**Alice Lexi Eddie Zack
The Famous Four!**

It was properly autumn when we drove up the hill to George's house, but it wasn't really cold at all, even though it was late October. As we arrived at the big glass house, I could see Zack was already there with his mum. Otter too. Zack got him back a little while ago because his mum spoke to Pippa who said she'd come and see him during the day. So Lexi and Hannah, who were looking after him, brought Otter back which made Zack really happy.

'I went out in that one last week,' Zack told me, pointing to a little silver sports car. 'And me and George had to change the tyre on the way back, look,' he said, holding out a bruised hand where he'd hit his thumb with a spanner.

He showed me the car that he'd slept in and the motorbike and sidecar, but my eyes kept going back to the plane.

'Are you ready?' I asked.

'Ready as I'll ever be,' he said, looking excited. 'Black Mountains.' He pointed out of the open door and towards the sea. 'That's where we're headed.'

I watched him race out of the building to George and I went over to Mum, Dad and Rebecca. I looked down into her pram and pulled one of the faces I know will make her laugh and she did.

'Have you wished him luck?' my mum asked and I ran over to the plane.

'Zack! Zack!' I shouted as he climbed the steps into the tiny cockpit. 'Good luck, Zack!' I shouted as George fastened his seat belt. 'You're the bravest,' I called as the engines roared into life, and Zack grinned back at me and shouted something, but I couldn't hear him.

As the little plane started to move, he pointed at his chest and shouted down again.

'Me tiger! You moth!'

38

Zack

The night we had our moonlight swim was amazing. I didn't tell Alice, but when we first got down to the beach I was a bit scared of swimming in the blackish-looking water. Even though the sky was lit up with the biggest moon I have ever seen, I was a bit nervous of swimming in water that was so dark. But when I watched Alice tear off her dressing gown and race for the water I knew it would be all right and afterwards Mum told me that Dad would have been terrified of swimming in the dark too.

When Mum said that Hannah, Lexi and her friend Eddie were coming to visit, I groaned, remembering how annoying they were last time. But when they arrived and brought Otter I hugged him tightly.

'Surprise!' Mum said and I kissed her cheek. What was even more surprising is that Otter has learnt a few new tricks from Eddie and Lexi, but he still chews stuff. I wasn't sure I really wanted to camp out with a bunch of girls, but I think I'm realising that girls can be pretty cool too. And Eddie has this really weird memory which I think is the coolest thing ever. She can remember everything she reads. Not just a little bit, *everything*.

After the swim, we stayed up really late and I laughed so much that my stomach kind of hurt, and in the end David had to come outside and tell us to be quiet. I don't know which one of the girls was snoring, but it sounded a bit like a baby pig and I was having the best dream ever when a noise woke me up. It sounded like crunching or chomping and my heart almost stopped when a large black shadow passed by the tent. At first I didn't move, hoping that the thing had been a dream, but the chomping noise started again and this time it woke Alice up. Just as she opened her eyes, the big black shadow moved past the other side of the tent.

'Oh my God, Alice,' I whispered, 'what the hell is that?'

But Alice smiled. 'Shh,' she said, holding a finger to her lips and climbing carefully over Lexi's feet to the end of the tent. 'Don't be scared.'

I felt my heartbeat get faster and faster as Alice slowly unzipped the tent.

'Be very still and as quiet as quiet can be,' she whispered into my ear. We inched closer to the gap and saw the moon-lit garden as bright as before, but nothing out of the ordinary. Then we heard it again. *Chomp, chomp, chomp.* I looked back at Alice with worried eyes, but she edged closer

237

to the gap, tugged on my T-shirt and pointed. I leaned closer and turned my head so that I was half in and half out of the tent. My eyes scanned the wall, the roses, and then it came into view.

'Wow!' I gasped. 'Wow.'

Outside there was a baby deer! I watched the young stag lean into a rose bush and bite off one of the flowers.

'They love roses,' Alice whispered.

We watched it for ages, eating rose after rose, until it was as though it felt us watching and it slowly turned to face us. It tilted its head to one side and the moonlight lit up its antlers so that I could see they had a sort of fur that kind of sparked in the light on them. I looked back at Alice and smiled, and the stag walked right past us, so close I could almost reach out and touch its fur.

'It's called velvet,' she said.

It made a little snuffling noise as it went past us and I watched in amazement as it leapt silently over the wall and disappeared.

The day George and I went up in his little plane it felt completely different, but it was like Dad was with me the whole time. The rain started in October and it didn't really stop. The snow came in December and the roads were so icy that even Otter sort of skidded across the little stone bridge. When Mum and I are out all day, Pippa comes over to stroke his ears and give him some food. He's already chewed my new guitar, but I don't mind.

I know that I've only been at the new school for a little bit, but it's kind of good and, even though I've made loads of new friends, I still can't wait for the next holiday. I especially can't wait for it to be summer. I can't wait for us all to be together again. I can't wait to go back to Culver Manor and the secret beach that lies beyond the garden door.

Epilogue

I was ten years old when I flew across the Irish Sea for the first time. I was twelve years old when I flew across the English Channel, landing safely and in time for dinner. I was thirteen years old when I was flown in a bigger plane across the Atlantic and the landing that time was pretty hairy, but I loved it anyway. I love each take-off. I love the feeling as I fly above the ocean. Each trip makes me feel closer to somewhere new and unexplored. It always feels like I'm the first person to see the shore, as though it's me that has discovered a new land for the very first time. Each time I plan a new trip, it's the beginning of an adventure. Each time I leave, it's exciting. It's both exciting and completely terrifying, but I love it.

I'm fifteen years old today and if I make it down safely I'll be the youngest person to have ever circumnavigated the globe twice all by myself. If I make it before six pm, I may even break the record. I've had a lot of luck on this flight. The weather has been just perfect. On the cockpit there's a good-luck charm that's made of tiny pink and white shells. *'Keep them close,'* she'd said to me and I had kept them close for three months straight. They've never left my sight.

In my pocket is an unopened letter that burns a hole in my chest. *'Don't open it until you land in Sydney. Don't you dare read it until you get there in one piece,'* I'd been told. *'Promise me you won't read it until you've made it there safely?'* I had nodded and crossed my heart, tucking the small white envelope into my inside pocket.

I'm circling the runway now. I can see the valley below and all I have to do is land her. 'Straight down the middle,' that's what George says, and as I drop down lower I have the sensation of a victory. I've nearly done it. I feel myself get lighter and lighter as I steer her closer to the ground. Straight down the middle. I close my eyes with a smile as the wheels screech upon the tarmac. I feel my racing heartbeat begin to slow down as I turn the nose of the plane to face the towers. I've made it.

I turn the roaring engines off and I can see them all running out to greet me. Cameras are flashing, people are cheering, but I haven't seen her face. As I wait for her to come into view, I reach into my pocket and pull out the small white envelope. I look down at the familiar handwriting and tear it open quickly. I hear the voices getting closer, they're shouting out my name, and carefully I unfold the letter. I read the words not once, but twice and I understand. I trace my fingertip along the looping letters and I smile. I read the words once more, my throat tightens and a tear falls upon the paper. Just six words.

You tiger, me moth. Love Zack

And, as I step out of the plane into a wall of heat, I see her racing up the runway to greet me. I push away the crowds of shouting people and I open up my arms. There she is. There's my little sister.

There's Rebecca.

Acknowledgments

Super special thanks to my amazing friends Rebecca Winters, Nicola Kerry and Alexandra Hemming. You are acefabbrill times eleventy million.

Thanks to my first editor Emma Blackburn who started everything.

Thank you Alan for once again steering me in the right direction. Thank you Roisin Doherty for helping me chose some very important details for this story. Thank you Luke Aaron Moore for helping me with Zack and for being rather hilarious. Thank you Ellie Ryhmer for looking after my boy so I could write more werds.

Thank you Sophie and Jane for your bestest brilliantest help.

Turn the page for a special extract of

Suzi Moore

LEXI LAND

Secrets uncovered, mysteries unravelled and a friendship to last forever.

My sister died on March the first which was really annoying because it was my birthday.

It was *our* birthday. Laura was my identical twin.

It happened very quickly and the doctor said, 'It didn't hurt.' I said, 'At least she got to open all her presents first.' Mum didn't think that was funny. I told her that I wasn't *trying* to be funny, but I thought that, if it had been me, if *I* had choked on a slice of birthday cake, if it had been *my* very last birthday *ever*, I would have *at least* liked to have opened my presents first.

But, that doesn't really matter now, because I don't like birthdays any more.

I don't like Christmas any more either. We've had one Christmas without Laura and my mum was miserable. She cries a lot now. My parents argue a lot and my little brother, Rory, talks to the wallpaper.

Sometimes, I hear my parents shouting late at night and once I heard my mum say, 'Emma [that's me by the way] looks so like Laura that some days I find it hard to look at her. Sometimes, I think I'm looking at a ghost.'

The morning after that I went into the bathroom and, using the sharpest pair of scissors I could find, I cut off all my hair. *All of it*. But I couldn't reach the back so I was left with two dark brown tufts. I thought they looked a bit like mouse ears, so with a black felt tip I drew a black nose and six whiskers on my face. I showed Rory and he laughed so loud that Mum came into the bathroom to see what we were doing.

MUM: Oh my God! What have you done?

I wriggled my nose and smiled.

ME: Squeak! Squeak!

Rory was still laughing.

RORY: I wanna be a mouse *too*, Mummy! Can I? Can I? Please?

But Mum just cried and cried.

ME: What's wrong? Do I *still* look like a ghost?

So this year I'm changing my birthday. I've decided that from now on I'll have my birthday on a different day in a different month. This year I will have a happy birthday. Mum won't cry and I'll have a proper birthday cake, not another weird sorbet cake, like the one we had to have for Rory's birthday. Apparently, you can't choke on sorbet and pretending to choke on it is 'not very funny at all'.

If I want to change my birthday the first thing I'll have to do is ask my parents. No, I won't ask them, I'll just tell them.

<u>At breakfast</u>

ME: I'm changing my birthday from the first of March.

DAD: Oh really? Are you going to change your name as well?

ME: Yes. You can call me . . . Supreme Lord Ruler of the World.

DAD: So, Supreme Lord Ruler of the World, when do you want your birthday to be? November?

ME: No. Too close to Christmas.

DAD: August?

ME: Too hot and besides everyone is on holiday in August.

DAD: Everyone? And why does that matter anyway?

ME: Duh! A party is pretty dull if it's just you and a balloon, Dad.

DAD: I see, and it wouldn't have anything to do with the amount of presents, would it?

ME: Erm . . .

DAD: Friendships should be about more than what your friends can give you.

ME: But what about what you said last Saturday night?

Mr Henderson brought you a bottle of wine and you said you wouldn't clean the dog's bowl with it.

DAD: I said that?!

ME: Very loudly, or so Greta says. Greta the Great. Thanks for that, what I really needed was to upset the popular girl at school's dad.

DAD: But you didn't say anything! It was me!

ME: Dad, in my world, what you do *is* what I do. If you're mean about someone else's Dad . . . well, I might as well have jumped on the lunch table in a tutu and told the entire school that I still play with Barbie.

DAD: Oh.

So, I'm having my birthday on a different day this year but I just haven't decided when. I'm looking for a sign.

I've already ruled out November, December and August. I can't have it in May because that's my mum's birthday month, June is Grandma's, October is Rory's, January is Grandpa's, February is Aunt Shelly's and my dad's birthday is in September. Which, only leaves April and July. It's the middle of February now, so I've got time to decide, and if I can't decide by the end of March I'll toss a coin instead.

At bedtime

MUM: I hear you're changing your birthday.

ME: Old news.

MUM: Soon you'll be telling me you want a new name too.

ME: No. But I know what I want for my birthday.

MUM: What?

ME: New parents.

*   *   *

I've made up my mind. My mum says that when I've made up my mind about something, nothing will ever make me change it again. Sometimes she'll laugh and say, 'You're just like your father. You're as stubborn as a mule.' But I don't mind. I like it when she says I'm like my dad, because even though you are not supposed to have favourites, I think my dad really *is* my favourite.

Anyway, I have made my mind up and my new birthday is going to be on July the fifth. Well, I only had two months to choose from. July the fifth it is.

In the car

DAD: Why the fifth?

ME: Er . . . because my name begins with E and E is the fifth letter in the alphabet.

DAD: Oh.

He looked very disappointed and said that it was 'a very unimaginative explanation'.

I didn't want to tell him that the number five was Laura's lucky number.

I didn't want to tell him that sometimes if we were sharing a bag of sweets, Laura would count them out and even if it meant I got more than her, she would always just count out five for herself. Five Skittles, five Maltesers, five Haribos.

Always five.

July the fifth it is. I've circled it on my calendar. Mum doesn't know it yet, but I've changed the date on mine and Laura's birth certificates too. I figured if I was having a new birthday then Laura would want one too.

*

Last night I couldn't sleep. The bed felt lumpy and my eyes just wouldn't stay shut. Maybe it was because Mum didn't come in and say goodnight. She was in *another* mood. 'Dark times' my dad calls it. Well, I wish he'd switch the light on.

I lay there for a long time trying to decide if Greta was right about my haircut. She'd told me at school that even though some of it has grown back, I still look a bit like Shaggy from *Scooby Doo* and I told her that, if we were talking about cartoon characters, she looked a lot like Marge Simpson. I didn't mean to make her cry but everyone said I was being nasty and it wasn't her fault that the swimming pool had turned her hair a funny shade of blue.

I had to spend the rest of the lunch-break sitting on my own, pretending to read a book while Greta and her friends sat by the fire escape staring at me and laughing. The more they laughed and pointed, the more I pretended that the book was the most amazing thing I had ever read – which wouldn't have been so bad had it been the right way up. So I sat there staring at the upside-down pages of my brother's library book and in the end decided that *Rocky Robin and The Rabbits* was much more interesting the wrong way up.

Anyway, I was trying to go to sleep and had just turned on to my stomach when I heard a rustle followed by a very familiar sigh. Then a voice.

VOICE: *July? Why July?*

I lay there completely still. Perhaps it was the telly. Perhaps my mum was talking on the phone. After a while I decided that I had imagined it and I was just drifting off to sleep when I heard a little cough.

VOICE: Er, hello? *Why July?*

I felt my skin prickle and my heart beat a little faster; this time I knew I had not imagined it.

ME: Laura?

VOICE: Yes – Laura, who else would it be?

ME: Is that really you?

The voice went quiet. Perhaps I had been dreaming. Stupid me, I thought. Now I'm hearing voices.

VOICE: Sort of.